ALSO BY TIM KRABBÉ

*The Vanishing*

# THE CAVE

# THE CAVE

## TIM KRABBÉ

*Translated from the Dutch by Sam Garrett*

FARRAR, STRAUS AND GIROUX

NEW YORK

*Farrar, Straus and Giroux*
*19 Union Square West, New York 10003*

*Copyright © 1997 by Tim Krabbé*
*Translation copyright © 2000 by Farrar, Straus and Giroux, LLC*
*All rights reserved*
*Distributed in Canada by Douglas & McIntyre Ltd.*
*Printed in the United States of America*

*Designed by Cassandra J. Pappas*

*First published in 1997 by Uitgeverij Bert Bakker, the Netherlands,*
*as* De grot
*First published in the United States by Farrar, Straus and Giroux*
*First edition, 2000*

*Library of Congress Cataloging-in-Publication Data*

*Krabbé, Tim.*
*[Grot. English]*
*The cave / Tim Krabbé*
*p. cm.*
*ISBN 0-374-11978-3*
*I. Title.*
*PT5881.21.R26 G7613 2000*
*839.3'1364—dc21*                                    *00-035344*

*The publisher is pleased to acknowledge that publication has been*
*made possible with the financial support from the Foundation*
*for the Production and Translation of Dutch Literature.*

# THE CAVE

## 1. *To Bring a Bag to Ratanak*

AFTER ABOUT A KILOMETER, as he'd been told, he saw it. A wide concrete building five stories high, back off the road at the airport's edge. In front of it was the parking lot. A few cars stood glistening in the sun. A fence separated the lot from a field that ran right up to the road, with low bushes, trash, the remains of crumbled walls and, in the middle, a lone, crooked palm.

Above the entrance to the building were words written in indecipherable curls, but he knew what they must say: BUILDING OF FRIENDSHIP BETWEEN RATANAKIRI AND VIETNAM.

At eleven he had to be at that lot.

The fear rushed in his blood like an infatuation.

SUDDENLY, the minibus taking Egon and a few other guests to the Holiday Inn drove into Ratanak: a swirling, honking sea of white shirts, scooters, bicycles, cycle-rickshaws, minibuses, delivery trucks, filling the boulevards from curb to curb. Along both sides were smaller eddies of ghost-drivers who hadn't dared to cross to their own halves. Everything was trying to honk everything else aside, and Egon's van, honking incessantly itself, swung through it all, thumping over gaping holes in the pavement, missing oncoming traffic by a hair. Everything was carrying something: baskets, madcap stacks of wood, clusters of live chickens with legs lashed to handlebars. In cycle-rickshaws were ladies and their daughters in pretty blouses; in a chair on a handcart was a silent old woman. In a flash, Egon saw a rat in the middle of the road, immobilized, its haunches already crushed, waiting with terrified eyes for the wheel that would put a finish to it. A few of Egon's fellow passengers, including the man in the white hat whom Egon had suspected of being his convoy ever since that morning in Bangkok, were taking pictures. He should be doing that too, but the parking lot paralyzed him.

Along the sidewalks were little stands, most of them with signs in curly letters, but there were also a few he could read, for HOT TOCS and POKKA, THE NUMER ONE DRINK IN RATANAKIRI. Laughing boys played at pool tables, and everywhere men were squatting in puddles of oil, amid wheels, exhaust pipes, gears, and gas tanks, like the remains of a routed, butchered army of scooters. The side streets were open garbage dumps, with pigs, chickens, naked children, women with yokes. And everywhere, covering entire sides of buildings, was the portrait of General Sophal, Worker Number One, lord and master of Ratanakiri. Always the same portrait: Sophal, twenty years younger than he was, strict and benevolent, a grave god, a mild murderer in a sparkling white-and-green uniform set against a fiery red background—the national colors. The portraits were the only thing immaculate about Ratanak; they were probably touched up as often as Sophal's uniforms went to the cleaners.

At a square, the minibus got caught in traffic, right across from a huge billboard showing a crudely drawn syringe with a thick red cross through it.

"Ratanak only three traffic lights!" the driver laughed. "All kaput! Finish!" But he tore loose and they were off again, carried along on all the insane off-and-moving, this flow of irrepressible, buoyant life. And in the midst of it, Egon and his bag, like a deadly virus in an exuberant bloodstream.

He wondered whether the other one was already in Ratanak.


HIS ROOM on the sixth floor of the Holiday Inn looked out over the Tonlé Kong, the Great River, calm and gleaming, a kilometer wide at this point. Here and there were clusters of little boats, hundreds of them, with thatched roofs like floating Gypsy caravans. When he opened the door to the balcony, the heat, which he'd forgotten about for a moment, rolled over him like a drop of amber that would hold him forever. He backed inside and closed the door.

On a low table at the window lay a folder with girls' faces and telephone numbers. The clock radio beside his bed said it was a quarter past one. Less than ten hours left.

Suddenly Egon was crying, although he caught hold of himself after the first sob, so he wasn't sure it could really be called crying. He sat down on the edge of the bed. "Aaah! Aaah!" he said. Something pressed against his chest, again and again, like an airbag, blow after blow. He rocked his upper body back and forth, looking at the suitcase he'd put on a chair.

Damn it, I'm hyperventilating like some old woman, he thought, what were the things that made me cry? There were three.

He undressed and went into the bathroom. Under the shower he tried to recall what those three things were. The humiliation of trying to make money this way, which was worse than having no money at all. The sense of being lost, here in a city full of creatures with whom you couldn't exchange a syllable. The relief of having made it through customs—he'd almost fainted when the nod came for him to move on with his suitcase. The horror at having made it through customs. They knew everything, as though the warning on the immigration card, RATANAKIRI—20 GRAMS—DEATH, had been stamped on his forehead. They had let him go on his way, the man in the white hat kept an eye on him, and at eleven they grabbed him, along with the other one. The unshakable feeling that this was the last day of his life. The river flowing there, not knowing a thing about him. That he'd let a bastard like Axel van de Graaf dictate his life.

He could give everything as a reason.

He was further from everything than ever.


THERE WERE no taxis in Ratanak, the girl at the desk said. If he wanted to go somewhere he could take the hotel shuttle bus. He'd just missed it; the next one would leave in forty-five minutes. If he didn't want to wait he'd have to walk, or take a scooter-taxi.

"But I wouldn't recommend it, not if you value your life."

"I don't value my life," he said.

His shoes hurt, his head hurt, his mouth was dry as he crossed the dusty plain between the hotel and the Presidential Palace. It was like walking through a desert. He'd have to buy a hat.

In the middle of the plain was a fountain with people around it. A wedding party, he saw when he got closer, with bright parasols; a young bride in a white gown with train, a groom in white tails, both trimmed with red ribbons and rosettes, were posing at the fountain's edge, surrounded by laughing family members clicking cameras. Egon took a picture, too, and the couple gave him a shy, proud smile. The fountain was dry.

Exhausted, his whole body hurting, he reached the palace. Behind the fence was an enormous portrait of Sophal. There were a few tourists. You could visit the palace, and he would, but first he had to get a car. He took a few pictures, then crossed to the streets on the other side of the palace grounds. The apartment buildings there were blackened, neglected to the point of collapse, the verandas spilling over with upturned tables and loose sheets of corrugated iron; brown stripes ran down the walls, as though they too served as drains—but the shadow they threw was divine. He'd wondered how he would recognize the scooter-taxis, but they recognized him; two, three riders were already stopping in front of him. He shooed them away; he had to drink something first.

Along a thoroughfare he found a kind of café, a shop with a few tables and chairs on the sidewalk, beneath a corrugated iron awning. From inside came the sounds of a television set, the battle cries of little children murdering each other at a video game. He drank three beers, one after the other.

Just as it occurred to him that he hadn't seen the man in the white hat for a while, he noticed another café-like establishment across the street, and a Western woman sitting under the awning there, alone, just like him. The successor to the man in the white hat? Nonsense; if anyone was keeping an eye on him, it would be a Ratanakirian. It was actually comforting to see that woman there; it meant he wasn't completely alone after all.

Through the traffic he watched her, as if viewing a film with only a few good frames left. She glanced up at him, too, it seemed. Egon was expecting a man to come along, a man who belonged with her, but she remained alone. He felt an overwhelming urge to cross the street and talk to her.

After a few minutes she left.

When Egon got up to leave as well, he noticed he was slightly drunk; his legs were almost too heavy to lift. The streets he came to now were busier; he took more snapshots: market stalls with TIN-TIN IN RATANAKIRI T-shirts, a theater with garish posters for kung-fu movies, a monk in an orange robe on the back of a bicycle. Everywhere lay and hobbled, crept the disfigured, arms and legs torn off, with open wounds and filthy bandages; blind men; madmen with gazes that fell far beyond Ratanakiri— victims of disease and malnutrition, wars and civil wars, the land mines still lying everywhere—a carnival of harm and dog- ged life.

Egon stood at the curb; three scooters stopped right away. He chose an older man with a green cap, hoping the man would speak a bit of French. But when Egon asked him, the man didn't even understand the question, and he spoke no English either.

"Avis," Egon repeated a few times, "car rent. Car, auto." He turned an imaginary steering wheel, pulled out the scrap of paper on which he'd written the address. "Forty-first Street, forty-one. Four one!" He traced the numbers in the air, pointed to them on his note, and the man nodded and laughed happily at everything.

At last Egon climbed on the back and, without looking, the rider shot into traffic. Egon held on to the man's shoulders. They swerved through the tangle of vehicles, wavered for balance when they got stuck, so Egon had to put his feet down to help push, and then the man would take off again, all in high gear, the scooter yelping like a whipped animal. They wormed through openings that weren't there, shot past cars and bicyclists, barely missing them. The girl at the desk had been right: this was risking life and limb. But nothing could happen to him. Only at eleven o'clock could anything happen.

He should have asked that girl to arrange a car for him, of course. Just like him not to think of that sooner. They would have brought it to the hotel; he wouldn't have had to walk at all. But what difference did it make? The wind was blowing through his hair; his shirt flapped against his bare skin—it was wonderful, the first pleasant thing since Amsterdam. Riding on the back of a motor scooter, how long ago had that been? Wouldn't anyone change places with him, General Sophal, Axel too? He didn't even care that they seemed to be driving in circles. He started recognizing streets and buildings, and the man would just stop and then speed off, again and again, down more streets they'd already taken, hoping perhaps that Egon would suddenly tell him this was it. But when they got caught in traffic at the same intersection for the umpteenth time, Egon stepped off and handed the man a dollar, suspecting it was many times the actual fare. Another scooter pulled up right away, and that one, and the next two, drove him around and around. The scooter-taxis of Ratanak didn't know their way around Ratanak.

Acting on impulse, because he knew it wouldn't be understood anyway, Egon told the next scooter driver to take him to Tuol Ek, the prison. "Yes yes," the rider shouted, and the aimless wandering began all over again. When he finally found a scooter that seemed to know what it was doing, it suddenly shot down an alley too small for a prison, or even to be a shortcut to it.

He's going to kill me now, Egon thought. Well, here we go.

The alley stank; they crawled along, around potholes, past mounds of rotting garbage. A rat the size of a piglet scurried away along an ink black ditch—an open sewer.

The rider stopped and signalled to Egon to get off. And now, he thought. They were in front of a house on stilts, and in the darkness between the pilings lay oil drums and parts of scooters. There were also about twenty young people sitting around on chairs, in neat white shirts and blouses. One young man came over to Egon and the scooterist, and Egon realized this was an English class. His rider had come here for help, and the young man was the teacher.

Egon told him where he wanted to go, and while the young man was explaining to the rider how to get to Tuol Ek, the whole class looked at Egon, smiling and giggling. Egon smiled back. There were beautiful faces among them.

The teacher said something to the class, and they all laughed again, bright and cheery.

As they drove off, Egon wondered what the teacher had said. Perhaps: "This white man is very nice and friendly, and he thinks Ratanak is lovely. He wants to go to the prison." The children would always remember him.

Two scooters later he was there.

TUOL EK WAS the name of the neighborhood: there were fewer potholes in the road there, the big freestanding wooden houses looked less shabby.

He recognized the prison right away, from the television news a few months earlier. The white walls with rolls of barbed wire along the top, the crowns of the three palm trees in the yard behind, and beyond that the top floor of the prison itself. To the left and right were the red tile roofs of the two wings. In front of the barrier pole at the entrance, four soldiers stood with rifles at the ready. Above the gates hung a portrait of Worker Number One, with a caption that probably didn't say: I belong in here myself.

Cheerful shouts came from a little field beside the prison; a group of men and boys were playing volleyball.

Egon didn't dare to cross over—keeping the street in between, he slowly followed the prison walls. He felt seen through, as though behind those walls they could read his thoughts on screens, see what his plans were.

The grim guards, the wall with barbed wire couldn't obscure that in French colonial times, this building had been a lycée. Something of the blissful ignorance of what life would bring still hung here, like a smell that won't come out of a piece of clothing. Under the red roof to the right, fourteen-year-olds had vaulted the horse and swung on rings. Quite a few of them must still be alive—but how many would know that Ratanakiri beheaded its condemned prisoners here on Friday mornings? The number of heads that had rolled since General Sophal came to power and reinstated the death penalty was no longer kept track of in Holland; there the count had stopped at 441, the number drawn by Herbert Doornenbosch, that big, bony fellow, all too human in his homeliness, the first and as yet only white man Ratanakiri had dared bring to the block.

Perhaps the soldiers at the gate were the same ones who'd been on Dutch TV, made celebrities by Doornenbosch; the odd Dutch tourist in Ratanak would undoubtedly come for a look at this place of horror.

The roof on the left belonged to death row, where Doornenbosch had spent his final months. Between that and the former gym, Egon knew, was a round patch of lawn surrounded by a gravel path. It had been filmed once, from a crane with a tele-photo lens. The camera crew had been kicked out of Ratanakiri right away, but the images had already flown. The crane had been impounded, and the man who'd rented it to them was now inside, serving a five-year sentence himself.

Until the final minutes, the condemned man was kept in his cell on death row, in the building on the left. When the moment arrived, he walked outside, to the gym, around the lawn, along one of the gravel paths. Did they go to the left, or to the right? Was that part of the ritual, or did they just do whatever? Was it up to the condemned man? But then how did you decide? And how did you feel, walking there? Were you "besieged by thought," were you resigned, or just crazed with fear?

The grisliest detail Egon knew about Doornenbosch was that he hadn't asked for a pardon. Perhaps others had convinced him it was hopeless, or maybe he'd chosen not to rot away in a cell for another twenty or forty years. But Egon was afraid that by refusing, Doornenbosch had shown his fascination with this death; that such a horrific way of dying was something you could become curious about. Doornenbosch had been young, only thirty-nine, still in his prime, adventuresome, had been mar-ried three times, had lived all over the world. Egon had seen a picture of him taken the afternoon before he was executed. In that picture Doornenbosch looked serene, tired, and content at the same time, like someone who's gone through a serious illness and come out on top. Who is no longer as strong as he was, yet as strong as he can be.

Today was Thursday; taking Sophal's average into account, one or two men in the building there on the left would walk the gravel when the night was over.

Across from the entrance Egon paused for a moment. He was almost afraid to look, but between two of the guards he caught a glimpse of the gravel. He was shocked that the pebbles on which Doornenbosch had taken his final steps could be seen right from the street, but then the whole neighborhood here was cordoned off every Thursday evening, and remained so until late Friday morning.

A guard gestured with his rifle: keep moving.

As Egon walked past the volleyball players, he looked at his watch. Quarter to four. Seven hours and fifteen minutes to go.

A SCOOTER FINALLY brought him to a car rental—Hertz, not Avis. In his white Toyota, Egon blended into the insane traffic and, soon honking along with the rest, worked his way past the official sights: the Presidential Palace, the Silver Pagoda, the National Museum of Art, the School of Dance. Everywhere were beggars, few still in possession of all four limbs, little boys trying to sell postcards, and everywhere he took pictures. That was what it was all about, that and the ticket stubs. Doornenbosch had taken the same pictures, put together the same collection of tickets, but it hadn't helped. On the contrary perhaps; real tourists threw away their ticket stubs. Who would save something like that? Only those who wanted to prove they were tourists. And therefore were not.

Egon couldn't take in any of it—eleven o'clock was all there was. As if it already existed, the way a country exists before you get there. But at the School of Dance he actually looked. From the edge of a roofed-in floor paved with white and brown tiles, like a big chessboard, he and a few other tourists watched as unspeakably graceful barefoot girls in red and white danced the way flowers would, their hands and fingers like leaves. It was the first thing in Ratanak that had any harmony, that was in keeping with something higher.

At the Silver Pagoda he saw the man in the white hat, who gave him a friendly nod and started a conversation which revealed that he was Frank from Tallahassee, Florida, and that Egon might run into him that evening in the disco at the Hotel Concorde. If I go, Egon thought, but then it might be wise to be seen there as well. There was no man alone in Ratanak who didn't go to the whores. Doornenbosch had been there, too. And how else would he kill time?

After he'd completed his tourist rounds, twilight was setting in. He drove back to the hotel, and from there he set out on a trial run to the Friendship Building. At eleven he'd have to find it without a hitch, and he wanted to know how long the drive would take.

It's really true, he thought, I'm doing this. It's not certain that I'll be coming back.

Sticking to the broadest boulevards, he had no trouble finding his way to the airport. There, too, the roadside was full of little stands and eateries, sharp young men in sneakers and white shirts, women with checkered cloths on their heads, people talking and eating, smoke curling up from little fires. All this life had passed him by when he arrived; he had seen only the parking lot.

Across the road he could see the Friendship Building now, dark and squat, the lights of the airport behind it. There were still a few cars in the lot, and lights at a few of the windows. It was getting dark fast.

Strange, really, to choose such a visible spot. But then maybe not strange at all. It could all be over within thirty seconds; no one would have to see a thing.

And after that? He couldn't imagine anything after eleven o'clock. Tomorrow seemed as unreachable as a dream. He shook his head. I have to stop making that mistake, he thought. That's not what I should be afraid of. Tomorrow will come. This isn't the last day of my life. It's the last day of my life the way it has always been. But that's exactly what I wanted.

He passed the building, circled the rotunda at the airport, and started driving back on the other side. He saw the turnoff for the Friendship Building, a narrow concrete road. Ten meters away from it he still didn't know whether he'd turn in, but he decided not to. It was as if going to the parking lot now might ruin something that would protect him later on.

Driving back into the town, dark now except for the glow from little fires and white shirts, he laughed at his fear and self-pity. There was nothing to worry about. Doornenbosch had made the papers, but when things went well, it didn't make the papers and maybe that happened every day. Security had probably eased up; after Doornenbosch, who would dare smuggle drugs through Ratanakiri? And even if he *was* caught, by beheading Doornenbosch, Sophal had handed America a certificate of good behavior; *his* country didn't help to poison young Americans. The general couldn't afford and wouldn't need to execute another Dutchman. God knows how these things worked: maybe Axel had been here himself, had negotiated personally with Sophal. Maybe that one head had paid a sort of toll, and now Axel could do whatever he liked around here. If so, he also would have made sure nothing happened to Egon.

At eleven o'clock Egon would give his suitcase to the other one, and that would be it. Thumb his nose at everyone. Pop off to Ratanakiri, show a little guts, and you made forty thousand guilders. No problem. The way Axel did things. Never be afraid, take what you can get. Egon would drive back to his hotel, go to sleep, and early tomorrow morning he'd fly out to Ta Prohm, to the jungle temples. He wouldn't see a thing, just wait for nightfall. Then the plane would take him to Bangkok. Less than twenty-four hours and he'd be there! Drunk with relief and triumph, he'd jump and shout at still being alive, at the strength and guts he'd shown. Compared to that, nothing mattered. The money he could throw away—he'd build a new life on the triumph alone.

He realized he'd forgotten to time the drive.

IN THE LOBBY of the Holiday Inn, in the elevator, his corridor, his room, hard-eyed men in uniform were waiting—but they weren't there. The suitcase was where he'd left it, on the chair by the window.

The Tonlé Kong was dark now, only the glimmer and reflection of lights from the boats let you know there was a river down there. Egon pulled off his sweaty clothes and tossed them in a corner, took a shower, called the desk and asked them to wake him in an hour, then lay down on the bed. He was exhausted, but knew right away he couldn't sleep. Maybe this was what the hours before the execution were like; maybe then, just like now, you were slung back and forth between fear and indifference, almost from one heartbeat to the next.

After half an hour he got up. He put on clean clothes and left the room.

IN THE HUGE HOTEL dining room with its panoramic view of the river, robots were eating and robots were bringing their food.

He wouldn't be able to eat a bite in there. If this was to be his last evening, let him spend it in the thick of life. A waiter came over. Egon stammered something, knowing he wasn't understood, and fled, the way drug runners flee from dining rooms.

It was a little past seven-thirty. The heat in the hotel parking lot was milder now, almost pleasant. He got in his car and began driving around, looking for a restaurant. Farther up along Tonlé Kong he parked and walked the riverside walkway. Everywhere people were sitting around braziers on the ground; luscious smells entered his nostrils. He came to a pier on the river with quiet Asian music and voices coming from it, people, mostly Westerners, eating at the tables. But that kind of being together wasn't anything to be part of on your last evening, and Egon walked back to his car, drove on, lost his way in streets without a single light until he came to a sort of market, along a cinder road that wound back and forth across railroad tracks. Music was playing everywhere; he drove out of songs and back in again. Cords of colored lights were strung between little shacks and market stalls; around tables in the middle of the road, sometimes even between the rails, people were sitting and laughing; boys and girls called out to him gaily to leave his car and come over. Up on some of the tables there were chairs with young girls sitting in them, wearing beautiful, colorful dresses. Adults and smaller children sat and played around the tables. Those must be their parents and brothers and sisters, and the girls themselves were probably whores. He wondered how much they asked. A few dimes, probably. It looked cheerful, but the thought that they needed that money to make those lovely dresses, money he might not even bend down to pick up, made the whole thing pitiful after all. Young people and little children tried to stop his car, everyone shouted for him to stop, to come over, and that was what he wanted to do, and then stay forever, forget the suitcase, never go back—but he had to stand the test.

DOWN A SIDE STREET, just off one of the boulevards, he found an outdoor restaurant that wasn't too crowded. When he climbed out, two little boys with bright feather dusters raced over to him. Egon realized they wanted to clean his car. The cheeriness of the feather dusters made him sad. Before he could say anything, before he had even decided what he wanted, an angry voice came from the restaurant and the little boys ran away.

He sat down, the breeze from a fan on a vacant table ruffling his hair every few seconds. A generator hummed; inside someone was laying a cement floor. A girl came over to his table, but Egon couldn't understand her English, and he pointed to say that he wanted the same as the three unshaven young Westerners at a table nearby.

"Chnang Dey," one of them said. "Very tasty."

"If you like rat," said one of his companions.

"Rat's okay," one of the others said, "but I prefer cockroach myself. Ratanak is the cockroach capital of the world."

"Alone?" the first one asked.

"Yes," Egon said.

"Doesn't have to last long around here." They laughed, and Egon laughed with them. They were Australians; he'd already recognized their accent—Chris, Roger, and Mike.

"But watch out in the dark," one of them said.

"What do you mean?" Egon asked.

The young man drew the flat of his hand across his throat.

They're seeing me, he thought. This is what it looked like when Dr. Egon Wagter ate something at a restaurant shortly before the moment we've all heard about. Everyone will want to know, but no one will ever know, what it was like in the hours before that. They're seeing it, but when they read in the paper about what happened at the parking lot, they won't know that was me.

"Girls enough," one of the fellows said. "This here's Suzy Wong." He waved his hand at the girl who had taken Egon's order and was now pouring him a beer, dropping ice cubes into the glass. She smiled. "Suzy Wong does it for a dollar, up there above the restaurant. Aye, Suzy?"

The girl nodded and smiled again, and poured beer for the Australians too.

"But I wouldn't go with her, 'cause she's not pretty enough. You agree, don't you, Suzy?"

"Shall I translate it for her?" Egon said. "I speak a little Ratan."

The Australians laughed, but the joke turned out to be that one of them actually did speak a few words of Ratan. He said something in rapid, staccato Ratan syllables.

"Don't you want to know what he said?" one of the others said. "Fucker Number One can't get it up anymore."

"He's been here five times already," the first one said.

"Nonstop fucking around here," said the young man who spoke Ratan.

Egon's food arrived, a brazier with a sort of soup bowl on it, into which he was to toss the side dishes set before him on little plates, the Australians explained to him. He ate some of it for the sake of form, but he wasn't hungry, partly because he couldn't shake the feeling that the meat was really rat.

When he told them he was Dutch, it turned out the Australians had heard of Doornenbosch. The subject interested them. You could buy drugs anywhere in Ratanak; Sophal was the biggest dealer of all; he had billions stashed away in Switzerland. He just didn't put up with competitors, that's all. Doornenbosch had been a dope. At least ten Australians were locked up in Ratanak for smuggling more, but they were only doing a couple of years. Doornenbosch had simply forgotten to slip the right people the right money. But then, decapitation wasn't so bad. No more worries, and it took only twelve seconds.

"Twelve seconds?" Egon said. "Only twelve seconds from your cell to when your head is off?" That suddenly seemed awfully fast.

"No, after your head's off," the Australian said. "The head stays alive for twelve seconds, didn't you know that? You can think everything and see everything. Then you get a bit dizzy and you think: Christ Almighty, I'm not going to conk out here, am I?"

They all laughed, and the boys started talking about girls again, but just to show he was made of different stuff, Egon mentioned the little boys with the feather dusters. The fellow who knew Ratan set him straight—those little boys weren't eight like he'd thought; they were at least thirteen or fourteen. The Ratanakirian was small by nature, and malnutrition made him half again as small. And those feather dusters didn't belong to them; they rented them from a boss and had to bring them back at the end of the day. Their dream in life was to have a feather duster of their own, and maybe to be a feather-duster boss themselves someday.

After a while the Australians got up and left—they'd be seeing each other later, at the Concorde. Ratanak was a big city, but at night it was no bigger than the disco at the Concorde.

Egon glanced at his watch. Almost nine o'clock. Only a little more than a hundred sweeps of the second hand—and how quickly it moved! Suzy Wong brought him coffee; the whole meal cost two dollars. He handed her a five-dollar bill and gestured for her to keep the change. The routine in her gladness disappointed him.

THE CONCORDE WAS Ratanak's other luxury hotel. Doornenbosch had stayed there. Egon had driven past it a few times that afternoon, and now, after a few minutes of aimless driving, he saw the letters CONCORDE again, high and luminous atop the roof. At the back of the hotel he found a parking spot, and when he climbed out a young man came over to him, hesitant and limping, a busted straw hat in his hand. He had a wooden leg. Egon waved him away, but the boy signalled that he didn't want money, at least not yet; he would earn his reward by watching Egon's car.

Egon said something, not knowing whether he meant yes or no. As he walked away he saw that the boy was still standing beside his car.

At the door to the disco he had to push his way through a whole crowd of other beggars holding out artificial limbs, empty trousers legs and stumps, like merchandise. The doorman let them go about it for a second, then shouted for them to go away. Egon thought he'd seen most of them before, spread out among the sights of Ratanak. A couple of them pointed excitedly toward his car. Were they trying to warn him about the boy? Or were they simply competitors who felt passed over?

Let them figure it out for themselves.

THE DISCO WAS brightly lit. Big wooden propellers turned on the ceiling, live lizards clung to one wall, remaining still for so long that they looked like ornaments, but in a pattern too haphazard for that.

A girl perching on a stool at the edge of the dance floor got up and offered Egon her seat. He shook his head, but she ran her fingers lightly over his arm and walked away, leaving the stool to him.

The Australians hadn't arrived yet, but the man in the white hat was there. He and Egon nodded, a bit embarrassed, although their seeing each other here was not much of a surprise. There were more men like him, Westerners in their forties, most of them at the bar, and surrounded by girls. The other one could be among them, but Egon sensed that it wasn't so. It only occurred to him now: maybe there was no other one at all. Maybe he'd been betrayed long ago, a pawn in a game he knew nothing about. Paranoia goes along with this, he thought. The music sounded like Abba; it made him sentimental. The boy who came over to take his order started an entire conversation in quite decent English, chuckling and touching Egon the whole time; what country did he come from, how long was he staying, had he already seen the temples at Ta Prohm? Out on the floor a few of the girls were dancing with Ratanakirian boys, their steps repetitive as wind-up toys. Their cute little evening dresses made it seem even more like a high-school prom, with fathers who had brought their daughters and were watching the first few dances.

The faces of the girls, and of the Ratanakirian boys, were lovely, unspoiled, like in that English class. It was nasty to have to imagine that these faces also reflected sorrow at the atrocities of Ratanakirian history, and that these girls, however genuine their smiles, however differently their profession might be viewed around here, still had to bear the humiliation of having men like him be able to possess them for money they'd never miss.

In passing, a girl kissed him on the cheek, just like that, no further advances, and another girl with delicate features and a yellow dress that contrasted beautifully with her brown skin came and stood next to him, drawing her nails gently over his bare forearm, giving him an erection.

"You buy Coke for me?" she said. The last two words rose in a little flourish, making them sound like the French word for "ant," *fourmi*—the way a child would say it who wasn't completely sure it was the right word.

Egon nodded, a boy placed a bar stool next to his, and the girl climbed onto it. She said her name was Nancy, asked his, and the conversation ground to a halt. "Egon," he said very clearly. "Egon," the girl repeated, and then came the inevitable giggling over the hard Dutch *g.* She laughed each time he said it, maybe *Egon* meant "cowbell" in Ratan. When he asked her her real, Ratanakirian name, she didn't understand. She repeated everything he said. She put her head on his shoulder, gave him a little kiss, blew on the skin just below his ear, bit him softly on the cheek. She could have been twenty-five, but just as easily fifteen. Her head, up against his, felt like a little squirrel.

He pointed at the lizards, still frozen in place on the wall.

"Alive?"

"Yes, alive!"

"Dead?"

"Yes, dead!"

The Australians came in and nodded at him approvingly. More witnesses to see him as just another tourist in Ratanak, going to the whores—but whores, even thinking that word seemed disrespectful to these girls.

He and Nancy watched the dancers, she occasionally stroking his thigh.

"You come with me?" she said, and for a moment Egon was disappointed that this was all it was about. "Two dolár one time, tree dolár whole night." He pictured an English class, the children all droning that phrase. He would have liked to go with her, if only to see whether her ingenuousness would last all the way to bed. But it was almost ten o'clock. A shudder ran through him. The final hour had begun.

He shook his head.

She grew cooler right away. She stayed next to him, but craned her neck in search of a new candidate. Egon gave her a five-dollar bill and stood up; her surprised kiss missed its mark.

At the door he looked at the lizards on the wall. Come eleven o'clock, they'd still be there. They were already in the future.

THE BEGGARS CROWDED around him again, but didn't follow him into the darkness to his car. The warm air felt nice now; a breath of wind brushed against his throat. At the car he looked up with a start; a shape emerged from the shadows. The battered hat brought it back to him: it was the crippled boy who'd promised to watch his car. He'd done that. His eyes shone, submissive and dignified at the same time. Egon took out his wallet, but saw that he had nothing smaller than a twenty. He didn't want to brush off the boy with a few coins, and he handed him the twenty. The boy looked startled. It was a ridiculous amount of money of course, something like a month's wages for a civil servant. But what difference did it make at a moment like this? Egon climbed in and drove off.

Two minutes past ten. There were no detours left.

WITHIN A FEW MINUTES he had found his hotel, was back in his room.

The suitcase was on the chair where he'd left it. He set it on the bed, touching it for the first time since he'd arrived. He took out the carry-on bag and his old clothes and shut it again. Twenty past ten. There was just enough time for a quick shower, but as he stood under the water he was suddenly afraid of being late after all, and got out. He dried himself hastily and, still partly wet, put on the clean clothes he'd laid out. He called the desk, asked the time, and had them repeat it. His watch was right.

Ten twenty-two. He sat down in a chair beside the little table at the window and looked at the clock radio next to the bed. 22:22. He tried to think, but it wouldn't come. On the dark river, tiny lights were still burning, from ship's lanterns perhaps. He tried to count to sixty, to force the clock to jump to the next minute, but halfway there he stood up and grabbed the suitcase. Okay, he thought, here we go. Watch carefully now. This is how Egon Wagter left the room on his way to the parking lot.

He walked out into the hall and stepped into the elevator, where a married couple on their way down looked inquisitively at his suitcase. Why would someone be toting baggage around at this hour? Fortunately, a group of older people in rumpled coats were standing at the desk, their suitcases huddled in the middle of the lobby. Probably a tour group that had just arrived. No one paid any attention to him. When the bellboy came over, Egon let him take the suitcase and carry it to the trunk of the Toyota.

Careless, he realized once he drove away; the suitcase wasn't very heavy. The boy might have found it strange. Maybe

he should have put rocks in it. But it didn't matter anymore—
nothing could change what had to happen.

THE BOULEVARDS and apartment buildings were dark, but the
cafés and shops along the sidewalks were still open, with people
eating around low tables lit by candles and tea warmers.

It was quieter in the streets.

He soon found the landmarks he'd noted on his test run, and a
little later he was at the city's edge and could see the lights of the
airport. The stretch of paved road was still lined with life, roadside stands, laughing people playing games, little children. And
somewhere people were getting ready to meet him. Police, rob-
bers. Or just the other one.

A baby sound came from his throat; he'd gulped. It sounded as
if he were wearing a diving suit, with heavy layers separating him
from reality.

Across the road was the Friendship Building, now a broad
block of darkness against the lights from the airport. Maybe the
other one was already waiting. He could see no cars in the lot.

Seven minutes to eleven. He was early; he drove more slowly.

It was like getting ready to climb some weird, barbaric scaf-
fold for a ritual he didn't yet know, amid song, music, invoca-
tions. But the hot and cold baths of fear and indifference were
behind him. Now that he'd arrived at this hour of hours, he felt
wistful. This was how life had gone; nothing but this had ever
been possible. You had friendships, loves, without being able to
see how they would bring you to the moment when everything
was decided. He thought of the moment when they'd asked him
what he wanted to be, and for the first time he'd said "a geologist." And a geologist he'd become, but it seemed as if he

should have said: "I want to bring a bag to Ratanak." Everything was in place now; it had never not been in place. He was frightened and happy at the same time, as though approaching some fulfillment.

Arriving at the airport rotunda, he circled it and began driving back toward town. On this side of the road, too, there were fires smoldering, radios playing, little stands selling everything, and every shadow could be someone with a walkie-talkie, passing along his position.

It didn't matter.

There was the turnoff to the building. He took a deep breath and drove in. The road sloped down. To the left was the field, the fence around the lot, the opening in the fence to the left. He drove out onto the parking lot.

There was one other vehicle, a white van, just like the one that had taken him from the airport.

He pulled in a few spots down from it, his front bumper up against the fence, facing the field and the road. He cut the engine, clicked off the lights, rolled down his window. It was quiet. He looked at the lights from the road. He recognized the crooked palm tree in the middle of the field.

He looked at his watch. Two minutes to eleven.

Maybe the other one was waiting in that van. He climbed out, but didn't dare to walk over. He tried to see if it was moving, the way you try to see if corpses in movies are breathing. But he saw nothing.

It was quiet in the parking lot, a deep stillness made audible by sounds: a motor scooter, cars on the road, voices and music from the radios at the stands, a distant engine revving at the airport. A droning came up as well, low and quavering, like one of those Australian horns.

A shape moved across the field, an animal, or a piece of paper. God knows who knew he was here, out in the open with a suitcase worth millions.

He was completely lucid. The air felt light like on a first date.

Eleven o'clock. One minute from now he would know how this ended. Strange that you couldn't see even that far into the future.

Was the other one watching? From the van? The building?

A piece of paper rattled against the fence, a light blinked on and off at the airport—and suddenly he saw headlights pulling off the road; a car was taking the turnoff to the Friendship Building. Egon climbed back in his car and shut the door. He left the window open. The other car drove slowly and hesitantly past the field, along the fence, through the opening and into the parking lot behind him, then it pulled in between him and the van, its front bumper up against the fence.

The engine stopped, the lights went out. Egon didn't dare to look.

It was quiet again. Again he heard the sounds from the road, snatches of music from the radios. The horn. *Didgeridoo*, those things were called; now he remembered.

A car door opened and slammed shut. Someone had gotten out; he heard footsteps. A shape approached, walked behind his car, came to his open window, bent over.

"Nobody lives in Siberia anymore," a voice said.

It was a woman. An American, judging from those few words. She was hoarse; she'd had to stop in mid-sentence to clear her throat. Her voice was civilized, nice.

He looked, and recognized her. It was the woman he'd seen across the street when he stopped for a beer that afternoon, the one who'd glanced back at him.

"In Brazil there are forests," he said.

The woman sighed, crumpled, and fell to the ground.

It was quiet again. Egon couldn't see her anymore. The didgeridoo droned, a motor scooter sputtered past. Shapes were moving again across the open field, between the fence and the road, and now he realized they were shadows thrown by headlights. He tired to open his door, but it only went a crack, the woman was lying in the way. He slid over to the passenger seat and climbed out on that side.

She lay still, only her fingers moving, like sea anemones in still water. She was wearing a black skirt and blouse; a necklace was hooked over her chin. Egon knelt beside her. Her eyes were closed; her tongue moved across her lips. He pulled the necklace down and slapped her softly on the cheek, which felt clammy. It was strange to be touching the cheek of a woman he'd only seen from across the street.

She opened her eyes and looked at him.

"Sorry," she said.

"Are you all right?" Egon asked.

"Yeah."

"Do you know where you are?"

"Yes." She straightened up, remained sitting for a moment, then Egon helped her to her feet. She let him. Her breathing was slow.

"You'd better sit down for a bit," he said. She nodded, and he helped her into his car, on the driver's side. He walked around and climbed in next to her.

"I'm so scared," she said.

"Me too," he said.

"I've never done this before."

"Me neither."

"It's insane," she said.

"Yes," Egon said.

Her voice was reassuring, something from a world he knew. It was unbelievable; he was actually talking to her after all. Her hair was dark, her face sad and mocking at the same time. She was still very pale. She looked about forty. Her lips twisted in a grimace, as though some pain was passing.

"I saw you this afternoon," Egon said. "In town, isn't that right? I was having a drink, and you were across the street, having a drink too."

"Near the palace," she said. "I saw you, too. You were alone."

A great relief came over Egon, as though they'd become separated that afternoon and had now found each other again. She sounded relieved too. This was all so badly organized, he realized. Imagine if he really had spoken to her. Then they would have found out who they were, and that could have been fatal if one of them was arrested.

"Shall we do it?" he said.

"Yes," she said. She nodded.

They climbed out and walked to the back of his car.

They stood facing each other for a moment, looking at each other. It was as though the silence, the droning of the didgeridoo, the night sky, had dropped a dome over the parking lot, as though they were in a huge room where there was no time, and where there could be no one else.

Egon opened the trunk and took out his suitcase. Together they walked to her car. She opened the trunk, he put the suitcase in, and when she closed the lid again it hit her arm.

She let out a little moan; by reflex Egon laid a hand on her shoulder, and suddenly she was in his arms. She pressed against him, and he pressed himself against her. Their cheeks touched.

She was crying; her body shook. He was crying too, out of fear, but also from relief at having found her again, at having her with him, here in this dismal parking lot in Ratanak. Her cheek was wet. He felt her face against his, not looking for a kiss, but it became a kiss anyway. They kissed each other's cheeks, lips, soft and rhythmically, like a litany.

Go, he wanted to say, the only thing we should do here is go away. Save yourself. But he couldn't let her go.

She took his face in her hands and looked at him, shaking her head with a little smile.

"I can't believe it," he said, and she said something back, but their noses were so full of snot from crying that it came out unintelligibly, and they laughed.

They snorted hard, and he took her by the arm and led her to his car, where they sat in the backseat and held each other again.

It was wonderful, like a fulfillment, to feel her against him, to kiss her, be kissed by her, to taste her saliva, hear her breathing. He didn't know her name or where she came from, but it was as though he'd never loved a woman like this. There were moments when he could think, and then he singled something out of everything there was: her hand in his hair, her sighs, her cheek, her lips, and he noticed that her kisses were a bit clumsy, like those of a schoolgirl doing it for the first time, but that only made it more wonderful. In the midst of a kiss Egon knew it was the last, and that when it was over they would go away and never see each other again.

They let go. The droning became audible once more.

"I wonder if those were the right passwords," she said.

They laughed.

"I was scared I'd forget mine," Egon said.

"Me too! But maybe they *were* wrong."

"Yes, maybe we were supposed to do something completely different."

"Well, we are doing something completely different," she said.

They laughed again.

"Maybe we were supposed to assassinate General Sophal," Egon said.

"That was it!" she said. "Now I remember. We were supposed to go to the palace and bump him off. That's why we were sitting there this afternoon—to check out the neighborhood!"

"But what if we get caught?"

"They'll throw a big celebration for us. We go out on the balcony and the whole country comes to the palace to thank us and cheer for us. And then all those portraits of Sophal are taken down and they put up portraits of us instead!"

"King . . ." Egon said, and he was going to say: "King Egon and Queen . . . ," but he stopped himself in time.

She noticed. "Not so smart to know who we are, is it?"

"No," he said.

They went on fantasizing about how they would change the history of Ratanakiri, free the prisoners, receive reporters from all over the world, and Egon imagined how everyone back in Holland would see him, the liberator of a tragic land, with this sweet queen at his side.

"I love you," the woman said.

"I love you," Egon said.

They were quiet for a moment. "We have to go," he said.

"Yes," she said.

She straightened her blouse, fixed her hair. Egon watched. These were the last moments, but they were still together.

She smiled at him, a bitter smile, a tightness at the corner of her mouth. "Goodbye," she said.

"Goodbye."

He still saw her; he could still touch her. But she climbed out, gave him a little wave, and then he couldn't see her anymore. He heard her footsteps, her car door. In a moment she would start the engine. And then she would drive away.

Tomorrow he would walk past the temples at Ta Prohm and think of her. There would never be an hour when he wouldn't think of her. She was the woman of his life. But he would never know who she was.

But what if not knowing anything about each other was just nonsense? What was the risk, compared to the certainty that they'd never see each other again? How many seconds did he have to decide whether she was worth every risk? Should he get out, stop her, ask her name, where she lived, or, if she was already driving away, write down her license number?

He didn't know. He had to decide now.

Any moment now, he would hear the sound of her engine.

## 2. Friends

EGON FIRST SAW Axel van de Graaf one lovely, clear summer morning, on Platform 1 of Amsterdam's Central Station. His mother had brought him by tram, but he didn't want her to come farther than the hall, so that's where they'd said goodbye. Knowing she was watching, but without turning to look, he had climbed the steps, duffle bag over his shoulder, to the platform and the start of the Davy Youth Travels trip to a camp at La Roche in the Belgian Ardennes.

He had just turned fourteen and because the camp was for fourteen- to seventeen-year-olds he was worried he'd be the youngest one there. As he stepped onto the platform and looked around for fellow campers, he saw a group of children and adults standing at the foot of a scaffolding that reached to the roof. There were bags and backpacks on the ground around them, and a big crate with the Davy emblem they'd said he would recognize from the folders. But no one saw him; they were all looking up, and when Egon looked up too he saw why: a boy had climbed into the scaffolding. He was way up already. A counselor shouted something, but the boy climbed on, causing a jingling, singing sound in the pipes. It looked dangerous, and Egon hated to think what would happen if the boy fell.

"Get down! You'll kill yourself! We're responsible for you," the counselor, hardly more than a boy himself, yelled. But the boy on the scaffolding climbed till he'd reached the top, just below the roof. He stood there for a moment, his toes sticking over the edge, and looked down laughing. "Hoo! Hoo!" he yelled, and it echoed.

"Get down!" the counselor called again.

"What?" the boy shouted. "What did you say?"

"Come down from there! And please, be careful!"

"I'm coming!" the boy shouted. He walked back and forth a bit, jumped up a few times to touch the roof, and only then began climbing down, swinging scarily from pipe to pipe. From the lowest platform he jumped onto the Davy crate, and from there to the ground.

The counselor who'd shouted said: "Why did you do that?"

"I didn't see a sign saying NO CLIMBING," the boy said. "I wanted to see if there was one up there."

There was muffled laughter. For a moment the counselor was at a loss.

"Don't do that again," he said. "If you fall, the whole vacation will be ruined, for all of us."

Everyone looked at the boy. But he stepped past the counselor and came right up to Egon, as if he'd been waiting for him. He had a thin face, stringy dark blond hair, forceful blue eyes.

"Hey, I'm Axel van de Graaf," he said. "Who are you?"

————

IT WAS A vacation predestined for falling in love for the first time, and Egon did. When he thought back on it later, it was so many other vacations as well: the one when he'd first smoked and gotten drunk; when he'd first gone to bed with a girl, with *two* girls no less; the one that had made him a geologist—but in the long run it was mostly the vacation when he'd come to know Axel, the vacation he spoke of whenever people asked him: "Listen, this Axel van de Graaf, you know him, don't you? What's he really like?"

The two girls were sisters from Haarlem, Vera and Florrie Lanaker, seventeen and fifteen, who clearly wanted to be seen as sex bombs, and were, too. In the train Egon ended up sitting across from them, and when they got to Belgium he spent some time in the gangway with Florrie, the younger, watching the landscape shoot past and learning a lot about horseback riding and their father's patent office. But Vera's laughter when Axel leaned over to whisper something in her ear made Egon realize that if you could get anywhere with these girls, Axel, with that whispering, was miles ahead of him already.

There was also another girl, Marjoke Heffels, from Hilversum, who'd stood wringing her hands as Axel climbed down from the scaffolding, and who had been more or less the only one who hadn't laughed when he was rude to the counselor. She had funny wisps of black hair and looked serious all the time, but in the train she laughed in a funny, snuffling sort of way when she and Egon accidentally caught each other's eye—and so did he.

It was a long trip and almost dusk by the time two trucks dropped them at the Davy campground, a grassy field all to themselves on the River Ourthe, a little outside La Roche. Out of the big crate came the main tent, and out of two smaller ones the pup tents they'd sleep in two-by-two. And while the smell of noodle soup spread from some hasty cooking being done, and they were all helping set up the main tent amid the mist rising from the little river, Axel said to Egon: "You and me, okay?"

Later that evening, in their tent, Egon smoked his first cigarette. It made him a little wobbly and gigglish, and Axel said he'd put some hash in it. The next evening Axel had a bottle of wine he claimed to have stolen in La Roche. Egon had drunk wine before, but never so much. The day after that, on their way back through the little town after a long hike, Axel suddenly pulled Egon into a shop and told him this was where he'd done it. And while the shopkeeper stood right behind the counter helping a customer, Axel took another bottle of wine from the rack and walked out. Egon stood nailed to the floor. The shopkeeper looked at him. Egon grabbed a pack of chewing gum and paid for it, but once he was outside the shopkeeper came after him and made him empty his pockets.

"Don't let me see you in my store again," he said.

"No," Egon said, and as he spoke he saw Axel sitting on a stoop a little farther along, the bottle in plain sight at his side.

Axel was fourteen, just like him, the son of a hospital director from Hilversum, and he claimed he'd already done it with six girls, one of them a woman of thirty-two, the wife of one of his father's doctors. He was quick, high-strung, pushy, constantly spreading the fear that you'd miss something if you weren't around him, but also that a police car would drive onto the Davy field and arrest all accomplices to the wine theft. He was crazy about poker and taught it to anyone who would learn, and in the evenings, and sometimes during the day at the nearby swimming pool, the games ran on until the counselors banned them, because the stakes were too high, and because Axel had punched a boy who'd accused him of cheating. By then he'd won more than a hundred guilders.

If you wanted Axel to go somewhere, all you had to do was put up a NO TRESPASSING sign. Close to the Davy camp was a sign like that, at a municipal lot with storage sheds, trucks, huge spools of cable, and two little black towers—like some sort of upside-down saltshakers under which trucks could drive to be loaded. With what, it didn't say.

One time, as the whole group was walking past the lot and Egon wondered aloud what could be in those saltshakers, it was as if he had already seen what he'd set in motion. Axel ran right onto the grounds and began climbing in one of the shakers, and an angry man emerged from a hut. Kees, the counselor who had called Axel down from the scaffolding at the station, tried to calm the man, while Axel, balancing on the edge of the saltshaker, shouted: "It's empty! There's nothing in it!"

He climbed back down, let the man's scolding roll over him and then, with the few words of French he knew, managed to find out what the shakers were for: in the winter they held salt, to spread on the roads.

"Some people have a lot of nerve," someone said.

"Get some yourself," Axel said.

THEY TOOK walks through rolling fields where tanks from the Ardennes offensive still lay half-buried, went canoeing, swam in the little river and the pool, visited a cave, saw a falcon hunt at the ruins of the castle in La Roche, the grave of a Dutch poet who had died young, and around the campfire they talked about the war in

Vietnam and who was better, the Beatles or the Rolling Stones. During one of their walks a huge thunderstorm broke, with crashes that rolled from hill to hill and finally came so close, with such terrifying blasts, that the girls jumped into the boys' arms, Marjoke into Egon's, and they all took off running. They fled into a barn that shook beneath the blasts and the downpour. Inside it smelled of rain, sweet and earthy, and was almost as dark as in the tents when they went to sleep. Marjoke and Egon sat beside each other on upturned buckets, laughing at each other's laugh at every new crash; Vera and Florrie lay on their backs on a little haystack, straws between their lips. Kees was watching them. Axel climbed onto a tractor, got it started, and rammed the barn door.

That evening in the tent, after the gong for lights out, Axel said he was going.

"Where to?" Egon asked.

"To Vera."

"To Vera? Now? What for?"

"To fuck," Axel said, and crawled out of the tent.

Egon stayed behind, astounded. Here was someone leaving a tent, to go fucking. It was impossible, but he sensed it was true. How had this happened? He hadn't really noticed Axel around Vera that much. That had surprised him, in fact, because Vera was a real looker, and Axel was always talking about women. It had even occurred to Egon that maybe it was all bluff. But if it was true, then how had Axel talked her into it? Did it have something to do with that whispering in the train? Or that tractor? If so, then how? If he'd climbed onto that tractor himself, he still wouldn't be where Axel was now. And then: Vera! A girl of seventeen who recited the makes of cars in which boys had taken her to parties. A woman, from the looks of her. And Axel was only fourteen, just a couple of months older than he was!

Egon pulled aside the tent flap and looked out. It was misty dark. He saw the outlines of the main tent, lit for a moment by the lights of a car taking a silent curve somewhere in the hills, and the circle of little tents. Maybe he was seeing the spot where it was happening. It was unbelievable: Axel was fucking. Now. Vera was fucking.

Axel was back with surprising speed, a gleam in his eye, just two breaths away from the fucking. They'd done it behind the camp, he said, beside the path where most of the hikes started. Vera had tits you could get lost in. No, they'd made the date even before the thunderstorm. Nothing special, he'd just told her they'd meet at the path at eleven-thirty. No, he hadn't said they were going to fuck. What else would they do? Look at the stars?

"But why did Vera do it? Is she in love with you?"

"Don't ask me. Because boys are made to fuck with girls, and girls with boys."

"But what if Vera gets pregnant?"

"Then Vera gets pregnant. Not me. If you're going to jump out of an airplane, you better put on a parachute. Ever see a swimmer with a parachute? No, because he can't fall off anything. Listen, I'm going to get some sleep."

He fell asleep right away. Egon could see Vera lying on the haystack in the barn, a straw between her lips, knowing she was going to fuck that evening.


THE HILL ACROSS the river was covered in blueberries, and it was a tradition at the Davy camps in La Roche that on one of the last evenings everyone went out picking there in teams of two. Jam was made from the berries and, depending on the harvest, you got one or two jars to take home. But above all, said a boy who'd been to La Roche with Davy before, the idea was to give the boys and girls who'd fallen in love a chance to be alone together.

After dinner was finished and the chores were done, they decided who would go with whom. Egon counted on going with Marjoke, but just as he was about to approach her, Axel, who was going with Florrie, pushed Vera at him.

Carrying baskets, bags, and sacks, they crossed the river at the stepping stones, where the boys had to give the girls a hand to make the hardest jumps. They spread out across the hill. Egon and Vera climbed almost to the top. He saw the whole hillside below him, the Ourthe, the dam they'd built earlier that day, the camp on the other side where Maria, one of the counselors, was taking jam jars out of a box and lining them up on the long table—with little *ticks* if you listened closely. Egon caught a glimpse of Marjoke's head, at the bottom of the hill. She glanced up at him too, it seemed. He smiled at her, but couldn't see whether her look was a smile as well. Her head disappeared behind the bushes.

Egon and Vera picked in silence, stopping once in a while to eat a few berries. He wondered why Axel hadn't gone with her, and what she thought about Axel being with her sister now. Those two weren't anywhere in sight.

Now and then Egon looked at the downy tops of Vera's breasts, visible in the V neck of her sweater. When she bent over he could see a great deal more. Axel had seen those breasts completely naked. Had them in his hands! And with him, Axel's tent mate, so close by, Vera had to be thinking about that. From up close he was seeing a girl who was thinking about fucking, about how she had done that herself.

She looked up at him, two berries stuck to her fingertips, and for a moment it seemed she was going to put them in his mouth, but she put them in her own mouth. Her lips were black from the berries she'd eaten already.

"You've got a crush on Marjoke Heffels, don't you?" she said. "Why didn't you go with her?"

"I don't have a crush on her."

"Yes you do."

"How do you know?"

"It's written all over your face," she said. She squished a berry on his forehead, laughing. "She's a nice girl."

"Yes."

"And she's got a crush on you."

"No she doesn't," Egon said. He looked down across the hillside. It was almost too dark now to see a head sticking up above the bushes there. He suddenly felt very sad.

"What kind of a guy is Axel, really?" Vera asked.

"A crazy guy."

"Has he always been like that?"

"I don't know. I never met him before this vacation either."

"Really? I thought you'd been friends for ages."

"No," Egon said. "Do you have a crush on him?"

"No," she said. She stared into space. "Can you keep a secret? I'll kill you if you tell him. I do have a crush on him. Without even liking him. I didn't know that was possible."

They continued to pick until they could no longer see the berries, only find them by touch, and they heard Maria banging the gong down at the camp. At the bottom of the hill they all met up again and crossed the stones in the river, using their flashlights to help each other find the way. At the camp the berries were dumped into bowls. Axel and Florrie had the fewest.

Everyone laughed about it, Vera too, but Egon wondered what she was really thinking.

Together they'd picked four big bowlfuls. The campfire was lit, and when they were all sitting around it, Kees, who was only twenty-two himself, talked about sex. The blueberry hill and the sex sermon, it was the same old thing every year; they already knew that. Sex, Kees said, was a very natural and important thing in your life, and they were at the age when, each in his or her own way, they would find out about it themselves. Davy, as they had probably noticed, gave them a lot of freedom in that. But they should take it from an experienced man like himself—there was laughter—that there was more to it than fucking or not fucking. He actually used that word, and there was a little giggling. A hand brushing a cheek, going out rowing together on a lovely day, an unexpected letter, walking hand in hand along a river when you loved each other—they might not believe it now, but those things could also be a huge kick, a fulfillment, something that stayed with you for the rest of your life. Even more than the fucking itself. "That hill you all just came back from has only one top. But everyone can find their own way there."

Suddenly Egon noticed that Kees had been looking at Axel the whole time. Maybe that time with Vera hadn't escaped Kees after all. Axel didn't look back. Later, when the campfire began dying down, Kees went around the circle and asked them all about their plans in life. There was some snickering about the ambitious surgeons, pianists, and aerospace engineers in their midst. Vera wanted to be a fashion designer, Florrie a veterinarian, and Marjoke an archaeologist. "A geologist," Egon said to that question, for the first time in his life.

"And you, Axel, what are you going to do with your life?" Kees asked.

"Waste it," Axel said.

There was laughter, mostly from shock. It sounded hard and rude, not what a nice guy like Kees deserved. He stood there with his mouth open, tears in his eyes. It was the story Egon would always tell later, when people asked about Axel. Almost everyone then said something like: "Well, he did a pretty good job of it," and something along those lines must have popped into Kees's mind too, but he'd had the strength not to say it.

Sometimes Egon would get out the photos from that vacation, but when he did, he never pointed out Vera and Florrie as the first girls he'd been to bed with. And while people were looking at Axel, he would look at them, one dark, the other fair, both with sweet, open faces, or at Marjoke, who was in only one picture.

In their tent, Axel said he'd taken off Florrie's top. She had these fantastic tits, too. But she'd been afraid to do it there on the hill. So he had made a date again, with her. Egon didn't believe a word of it. But sometime after the gong had sounded, Axel left the tent again. Once he was outside, he stuck his head back in and said: "Come on, you take Vera. Otherwise she'll just be lying there by herself."

Egon suddenly felt as though he was dangling from a rope over a ravine. The idea of taking a girl just so she wouldn't be alone was completely insane, of a daring he knew would always be beyond him. And that "taking," what was that? Fucking?

"Come on," Axel said. "We'll go together. They're waiting for us. I already told them. These are fantastic babes."

Egon didn't dare, and he didn't want to. He wasn't even in love with Vera. But it was impossible to stay in the tent, the way you can't stay in your chair when sirens go wailing past your window. He crawled outside. The little tents stood in a circle, like dark Monopoly houses. A couple of oil lamps were lit under the awning of the main tent, and voices of the counselors, Frank, Kees, and Maria, could be heard faintly.

The two boys went into the bushes and cut wide around the ring of tents, Axel out in front. Egon was scared silly, like he was on his way to commit a crime. At the sisters' tent he thought: This isn't right. This shouldn't be. Vera and Florrie don't know a thing. Axel never even made a date with Florrie.

Axel went to the front of the tent, there was some hurried whispering back and forth, then he called Egon and they crawled in together. The very few times in his life that Egon told the story of his first time, he did so in words that filled the sisters' tent with laughter and excitement, that made it sound like fun. But it hadn't been fun. Vera and Florrie hadn't known a thing. They were probably normal girls, not sex maniacs at all, jealous of each other too, and they'd let themselves be bowled over, like he had, by Axel, by the peculiar authority of his charm.

The tent was so small that Egon couldn't help ending up half on top of a girl's body. There was a nervous hissing for silence, laughter. Irresistibly funny: people falling over other people. Axel had wine again, and they shared camping cups two-by-two. And then, while Egon was still thinking that at least one couple would go off into the bushes, Axel had simply grabbed his girl and started in.

So Egon had grabbed the girl on his side of the tent pole, too. Later he discovered that he didn't know who it was. The first few years after the camp he was sure it had been Florrie, but after a moment of doubt, because it would have been more logical for Axel to start with her, that certainty had never come back. Whoever it was, he remembered the moment of shock in the midst of the hot, shameful bumping, when something that resisted opened, she sighed slightly, and he fell in, locked immediately in a warm, strong grip.

He also remembered the sound Axel made, a sort of panting and laughing at the same time, and the strain in his girl's body, even as she went along with it, and the laugh she'd laughed now and then to make herself believe it was fun, the laugh of someone who shows up in costume at an ordinary party and decides to make the best of it.

He came, and Axel had probably come first, because he immediately began pushing away so they could switch girls. They crawled around to the other side of the tent pole, and went on with the other girl. There had been no more laughing then.

Axel came again quickly, with a high-pitched sound.

Egon was still going at the second girl when the flap was yanked open and a flashlight shone into the tent. She pushed him off her.

"What's going on here?" someone shouted. "Are you completely out of your minds?" It was Kees; behind him stood Frank and Maria. "Out of that tent, you two!"

"Fuck off!" Axel shouted. "What is this? Can't you even screw in peace at Davy? Hey! Get that light out of my eyes."

Kees was dumbstruck, the light shone on. Axel crawled out of the tent, stepped up to Kees, and knocked the flashlight out of his hand. It fell on the ground, the glass broke. A little spot on the grass was brightly lit. Vera and Florrie were crying. From the openings of all the tents, the whole camp was watching. Axel stood across from Kees for a moment, buck naked. Then he walked past Kees to their tent, straight across the field. Everyone watched him go, and when Egon crossed the field, too, he knew no one was looking, for all eyes were still on the tent flap behind which Axel had already disappeared.

IT WAS as though there'd been a death in the camp. The next morning at breakfast, no one said a word. Vera and Florrie sat close together. Egon felt disgust and admiration around him, but felt only disgust himself. He wished he were dead. He didn't dare to look at Vera and Florrie, and least of all at Marjoke. When he did anyway, she looked away. Axel was angry because someone had eaten all the chocolate sprinkles.

After breakfast they had to report to the main tent; first the sisters, then Axel and Egon. Kees told them they didn't fit in with the spirit of Davy. A letter would be sent to their parents.

"You're telling me two things here," Axel said. "I don't fit in with the spirit of Davy. That's right. My parents are going to get a letter. That's wrong. Because if my parents get a letter, Vera and Florrie's parents are going to get a letter, too. And that letter says you couldn't keep your hands off Florrie. That isn't true, but you would have liked to."

A stunned silence fell. "You'll go a long way," Kees said finally, shaking his head slightly. He held up the flashlight with the broken glass. "Are you going to have this fixed?" He waited for a moment. "No, I don't think so. Okay, you can leave."

Outside, Egon walked to the pump to splash water on his face and be without Axel for a moment. When he looked up, he was facing Marjoke. He was startled and she was, too; she probably hadn't seen him. He felt empty and dirty, robbed of something for good.

Neither of them knew what to say; all they could do was look at each other.

"It was Axel," Egon said.

Marjoke nodded, her lips pursed. "Will you be punished badly?" she asked.

"No," he said.

"I'm glad," she said, and walked away.

Egon prayed that Axel would take it easy for the rest of the vacation, and he did, except on the way home, when they had to change trains at Liège and Axel went into town despite strict orders, only to return after their train had already left. The whole group had to wait an hour for the next train. Axel showed Egon a bundle of Belgian money; he'd sold the rest of his hash in a café.

ONE EVENING at the start of his junior year in geology in Amsterdam, while he was with a few friends in a café, Egon heard his name shouted through all the hubbub. He recognized the thin, actually quite ugly face, the burning, forceful blue eyes, the spiky hair of indeterminate color, but most of all he recognized Axel by the feeling of unrest rising inside himself.

"Egon!" Axel shouted. "What was in the saltshakers?"

"Nothing," he said.

Axel hugged him, called for beer, asked how he was doing, told him how *he* was doing, dredged up old memories, pulled him into his circle of friends and out of Egon's own.

Axel had gone to boarding school for a few years, finished his exams with a little delay, and now he was a freshman in law in Amsterdam, a fraternity man, a "Grimmy Bear," as the members of his house, the Grim, called themselves. The house was at the edge of the red-light district, on the Grimburgwal—that's how they got the name. There were a couple of other Grimmy Bears in Axel's group, and an incredibly beautiful girl named Hildegonde. She was Axel's girlfriend.

Within a week Egon had become part of Axel's life, and that of the Grim. Axel may have come from Hilversum, may have spent years at a boarding school in the sticks and arrived in town only a month ago, but he already knew the Amsterdam café scene better than Egon did. They saw each other almost every evening in a few of the usual places, or at night in the Kopper—a series of catacombs on one of the canals, where a very different sort of young people came, and where a fatal knifing was rumored to have taken place—or at the Grim itself. The house on the Grimburgwal was a maze of hallways, little rooms, staircases, caverns, and cellars. It smelled stale, of beer and canal, and no one there ever wore a tie. Egon, who belonged to a progressive student club, had always imagined fraternity life to be quite different—but the Grim was not your typical fraternity, they assured him of that. Axel, the only freshman living at the Grim, had the smallest room, a cubicle with a desk and a bed and just enough room for a chair in between. You couldn't imagine anyone studying there, or anywhere else at the Grim for that matter. No one complained about the constant noise. A nonstop party seemed to be going on, always in the biggest room where the oldest Grimmy Bear lived, a fellow named René who was almost thirty and hadn't been to classes for years. But you always had the feeling that the parties were really Axel's. He was always there; he was the one who knew everyone, and everyone knew him. Those parties were packed, often sprawling into other rooms. There was always beer, for which the hat was sometimes passed, and often you smelled the sweet, caustic odor of joints going around. The partygoers weren't all university students, not by a long shot. There were people from the theater school, regulars from the Kopper with their short hair and motorcycle jackets, a young journalist from the offices of a nearby weekly, a couple of women who were said to be whores, a singer who'd already cut a single, and suddenly one night, slouching in the worn-out armchair in the corner, sitting amid the bottles on René's desk, were the members of a famous American rock group. And often there were two lumbering men with accents from the street, Jan and Faas, who were older than everyone else, always standing together in the same spot, their calm radiating some sort of danger. "What kind of guys are they?" Egon once asked the journalist, whom he talked to on occasion. "Oh, they're hoods," he'd said.

Axel was a firefly on those nights. Sometimes you wouldn't see him for hours, you'd wonder whether he was even around, and then the gleam in his eye would suddenly shoot past. Hildegonde was usually there too, but Axel took other girls to his room all the time. It happened just as mysteriously as it had at La Roche. You wouldn't see him talking to the girl, you'd barely see them in the same part of the room, but suddenly they'd be gone. A little later they'd both be back, shiny and defiant, the way Axel had come back into the tent at La Roche after being with Vera along the path. "Just showed Judy my room," he'd say, and now Egon no longer doubted him.

One time when Egon opened a door in search of his coat, he saw a couple of boys and girls sitting on the edge of a bed and on chairs across from it. He felt their mystery even before he saw the needle one of the girls was putting in her arm. He found it an ugly sight, and in his shock he closed the door so quickly that he didn't see whether Axel was there, too.

There was a strange atmosphere at the Grim, as if all kinds of things were going on that you didn't see and weren't supposed to see. As if everyone were something else, something you didn't know. Egon wondered if Axel was dealing drugs. He almost had to be: he never studied, didn't have a job, but he always had money. He'd done it back then, in Belgium. One time at the

Kopper, where Egon was always uncomfortable amid the constant roar of music, Axel had suddenly pressed a little packet in his hand and said: "Hold on to this for a minute." At almost the same moment, at least eight policemen charged in, and Egon had known he was going to jail for years. He was sick with fear, the little packet in his fist in his pocket like a hand grenade. The policemen frisked a couple of boys, Axel too, but not him. When they left, he gave the packet back, but was too stunned to be angry, or to turn down the hundred guilders Axel gave him. He didn't ask what was in the packet either, and Axel didn't tell him.

Egon decided to stop going to the Kopper. I should really break with Axel, he thought. That isn't the kind of thing you do to a friend.

One evening, late, while he was studying, his landlady came to say there was a call for him. She was a little perturbed; he'd promised not to let anyone call after ten o'clock, but the caller had said it couldn't wait. It was Axel, with a strange story. This girl, Margriet, had a crush on Egon, but she was afraid to tell him. So *he* was telling him instead, and he had arranged a date for them right away. She was expecting Egon at eleven. Axel gave Egon her address and hung up.

Egon didn't get it. It was already ten minutes to eleven! He knew this Margriet, not a particularly pretty girl. He'd seen her around the Grim and the cafés. Who would have suspected—he'd always figured she was after Axel but that Axel wasn't interested in her.

He hopped on his bike, rode to the other end of town, and was met with a hail of abuse. Margriet had a date with *Axel* at eleven. When she'd calmed down, she didn't want Egon to go away, and for a few weeks they had an affair.

———————

IN THE SECOND WINTER of Egon's Grim years, as he later came to think of them, he heard the rumors that Friso Lisse, a boy he knew from the entourage, had disappeared. He'd been gone for two weeks; no one had heard from him. Egon cycled past his house a few times, and each time Friso's scooter was parked in the same place.

Egon wondered if it had something to do with the Grim. It almost had to; you couldn't move in such shady circles and disappear for any other reason. But no one knew a thing. Then Hildegonde disappeared too. You never saw her in the cafés anymore, not at the Grim either. And Axel was a complete blank. He skirted any conversation leading in that direction. Maybe she'd broken up with him, and he was afraid to say so. But Egon heard that Hildegonde had stopped going to classes as well. The scene had suddenly become eerie and sorcerous, as though the Grim had trapdoors you could fall through and nothing would be left of you. If it had happened to Friso and Hildegonde, maybe it could happen to him. Sometimes Egon longed for that—to be like them, a mystery that kept everyone guessing, that filled everyone who had stayed behind with horror. When he brought up the disappearances, he sometimes encountered a strange hilarity, a looking-away. He sensed he was talking to people who knew the secret—but who they were, he didn't know.

One evening he decided to make Axel explain. He went to all the cafés, to the Grim, and finally even the Kopper. There two boys forced themselves on him and tried to sell him something, and when he showed no interest, they began threatening him. But suddenly Axel appeared out of the darkness and the boys vanished. Axel pulled Egon along to a bar in a far corner where he was sitting with a Chinese girl, and before Egon had a change to ask his question, Axel asked *him* something: was he interested in making an easy thousand guilders?

Egon felt the wind knocked out of him. Axel was suggesting that he disappear as well. That had to be it. If he said yes, he'd know the answer to the riddle.

"Does it have to do with Friso and Hildegonde?" he asked. He could barely think, barely speak.

"You go for it?" Axel asked. "Absolutely no risk. A thousand guilders!"

"What happened to Friso and Hildegonde?"

"Twelve hundred," Axel said. "Because you're my friend."

The Chinese girl smiled faintly at Egon.

"I have to think about it."

"Don't," Axel said. "Who'd be dumb enough to think when he's got a chance like this? Twelve hundred guilders!" He laughed, thumped Egon on the arm, and turned back to his girl.

Egon's mind whirled. He was shocked by how easily Axel had admitted to being involved in criminal activities. Because that had to be it—how else could you offer someone twelve hundred guilders, just like that? Egon didn't know what to do. Twelve hundred guilders was a lot of money, and maybe there really wasn't that much risk. Axel had let his girlfriend do it. Maybe Friso and Hildegonde were fine; maybe they just couldn't show their faces for a while. And it *would* be an adventure. Didn't Egon often think, during whole days spent staring through his microscope at stones that were millions of years old, that he longed for something more exciting, something that happened *now*—that being good wasn't everything? Was he a coward if he didn't accept Axel's offer—or stupid if he did it to avoid being a coward?

Just when he was about to go to the Grim and tell Axel he'd do it, he saw the answer in a weekly. On the cover was a photo of a stolid face he recognized immediately, despite the black bar over the eyes: it was one of those men, Jan and Faas, he'd seen so often at the Grim. This was Jan—Jan S., it said in the story, which was written by Michiel Polak, the journalist he'd occasionally talked to at the Grim. S., who'd been convicted a few times for pimping and possession of illegal weapons, was the kingpin in a ring of people smugglers. For a few thousand guilders, he had Dutch citizens, most of them students, go to Poland, Czechoslovakia, East Germany, and other Eastern Bloc countries. There they handed over their passport and went to the embassy to report it missing. If someone tried to leave the country with their passport and was arrested, they were later held at the border themselves. It had gone wrong any number of times: Polak listed seven young people from Amsterdam who were now in Eastern European prisons. Friso and Hildegonde were among them. They'd both received six months in Poland, but one girl was serving a two-year sentence in East Germany.

There was no mention of Axel or the Grim. "For a few thousand guilders"—Axel had offered him twelve hundred, told him there was no risk. Axel had lied to him, tried to make money off him, would have let him go to prison. He'd pressed the little packet on him that time at the Kopper; that could have gotten him into all kinds of trouble. He let you do things you didn't really want to do. Egon pictured Friso and Hildegonde in their cells, René, whose future was being partied away under his nose. The Grim had cost Egon at least half a year, too.

The moment had come to think clearly about Axel. He was fascinating, irresistible, a friend if you wanted to call him that, but first and foremost he was a bastard.

Egon decided to break with him.

HE GOT his bachelor's, became a graduate assistant, and, for his thesis, was assigned to do research on the great thrust faults of the Andes. He made several trips to western South America, learned to speak Spanish well, and reveled in the vistas on the plateaus, the villagers who accepted him as a strange sort of gold digger, the old Land Rovers he drove, the way the sun came up as he walked to his site, but above all he loved the work itself.

As he searched for faults, bridging tens of millions of years with one hand when he found them; as he hacked out stones, numbered them, wrapped them in newspaper and put them in his rucksack, as he had the village carpenter build crates in which to ship them home—it was like he was back at the moment when he'd first wanted to be a geologist and was longing for this. And the feeling continued when he was back home and, in the packing cellar of his institute, saw his stones again, hacked them to pieces and examined them, when he worked out his notes, developed his pictures—when he wrote. That there would be little for him to do after school but find oil for billionaires, he would worry about that later. This was wonderful. This was about the origin of the earth and life itself, about the perplexity of time. It connected him with back then, and he could only wonder at how he'd already felt this love before he could have known what it was for.

HE NEVER SAW Axel anymore. That world had vanished. From across a movie theater he once saw Margriet, the girl Axel had made him have an affair with, but he didn't go over to her. At a tennis court he ran into Friso, the boy who'd disappeared first. Egon could imagine he'd rather not go into that, but Friso brought it up himself. He'd spent four months in a Polish prison. That was four years ago, but he was still brimming over with the excitement of the trip, the horror of getting caught, the fascination of the characters he'd met in prison and the stories they'd told. He'd picked up some Polish and was thinking about taking a course so he wouldn't lose it.

"Ever see Axel these days?" Egon asked.

"No," Friso said. "In fact, I think he's doing time."

EARLY ONE JUNE MORNING in his last year at school, as Egon was cycling to catch a train for the freshman stratigraphy week he'd be leading in the Ardennes, as he was thinking back on the vacation with Davy Youth Travels that had set out from this same station eleven years earlier, he was startled from his reverie by the blast of a car's horn. Before he knew what was happening, the car had run him up onto the curb. He had stepped off his bicycle, half falling and half stumbling, and the driver had jumped straight out of his thoughts and into reality.

"Egon!" Axel shouted, just as he had in the café when they'd seen each other for the first time since La Roche. Axel was jittery, high-strung and speedy from a night without sleep. In the front seat, leaning against the door, was a girl, dead tired or drunk, or stoned. "Egon! How are you! Are you a professor yet? Is it late or is it early? What was in the saltshakers? Come on, let's grab some coffee."

Egon said there was nothing in the shakers, that it was good to see him too, he'd just been thinking about him because he was on his way to Belgium, but he didn't have time; he had to catch a train.

"I'll take you there," Axel said.

"It's only a five-minute ride. And I'd rather leave my bike in the racks."

"To Belgium, dummy," Axel said.

There was no way around it. Axel roared over you, making you believe that what you wanted was ridiculous and what he wanted was the thing to do. Egon could say no all he wanted, could consider that he needed the train ride to prepare himself, that he wanted to do some reading, maybe even look around La Roche or go to the caves at Hurennes, least of all with Axel—that he'd broken with him long ago—but his bicycle was already locked up, the girl was in a taxi, and they were already over the border.

It was funny to see a fourteen-year-old drive a car. Axel was keyed up, overbearing, exciting as always, but he'd changed, too: he was less thin and bony, and there was a new kind of confidence. No longer was he the gambler down to his last cent; he was a gambler who could afford to lose. He wasn't becoming something anymore; he *was* something.

What, that remained unclear. Everything remained unclear. Axel was no longer going to school, and he'd moved out of the Grim, but when Egon asked him where he lived, he didn't mention a street or an address, just a neighborhood. He was in business: refrigerators, television sets, cut flowers. Egon didn't believe a word of it, and it seemed like Axel didn't expect him to. He was a professional criminal now; he had to be. A drug dealer, hardened by a secretive and probably dangerous existence from which he'd impulsively taken this day off. He must have done it for the thrill of the moment, to be someone who did things like this—the drive itself, the day in Belgium, was the price he had to pay.

But still: Axel was someone from his life. A friend, whatever else you might say. That friendship was over, that had been La Roche and the Grim, but this belonged to it like an overseas territory. And just as the laws of the motherland are looser in such parts, Egon felt that today Axel would reveal more of himself than ever.

They arrived far too early in the village where Egon was to meet his students. On the market square, outside a hotel, they had breakfast in the morning sun. When they were finished, Axel took a room and went to bed. Egon had all the time he needed to prepare.

The rest of the day, while studying maps, tracing strata, dripping sulphuric acid, and answering questions, Egon thought about Axel and couldn't help counting the hours until he'd see him again.

When he got back to the hotel at five, Axel was still in bed. Half an hour later he came downstairs, rested but still tight with sleep. He barely seemed to notice Egon, and disappeared for another half hour to make some calls. He paid for everything from a wallet stuffed with hundreds, brushing aside the difference between Dutch and Belgian money with an enormous tip, and they drove off in search of a restaurant. Passing through Hurennes, Egon recognized the little station where they'd once stepped down, and where their hike to the cave had begun.

There was a cable car these days, he saw.

In the hills behind Hurennes, Axel found a gourmet restaurant where they could sit outside beneath the lindens, with an endless view of the rolling countryside. It was still early; they were the only customers. Axel ordered a bottle of wine, but drank only mineral water himself.

"That Kees," Axel said after a while. "You ever hear anything about him?"

"Kees who?"

"Counselor Kees. From Davy Youth Travels. You remember his last name?"

"No," Egon said.

"'You don't fit in with the spirit of Davy Youth Travels,'" Axel said, stressing each word, and Egon recognized the phrase. "I liked him," he said. "He was right."

"But not to butt in when you're making it with a woman."

"He was right about how it can be more special to walk through a park with a girl than to go to bed with her. It was pretty courageous of him to say that to a bunch of teenagers. I still think about that sometimes."

"He just wanted to get into their pants himself, that's all."

"But haven't you ever had that? That you're walking through the park with a girl and stars explode when you take each other's hand?" Egon had tried to find a better way to put it, but suddenly he sensed that the worst way he could say it was right for now. This was the moment. Maybe they had never been friends and only were now. This was the moment to take off your mask. Maybe those stars would make Axel realize he was doing that, and Axel would do it, too.

"You underestimate me," Axel said. "What you're saying is, you're more sensitive than I am."

"That time with Vera and Florrie. That was actually rape."

"What!" Axel said, sitting bolt upright, as though someone had thrown a pebble at him. "Goddamn it, Egon. I've been driving you all over Western Europe. Do you always call your drivers rapists?"

"They didn't really want to."

"Didn't want to? What do you mean? They did it, didn't they?"

"I didn't want to either."

"No?" Egon could see Axel was disappointed. "I sure remember that big white butt of yours going up and down beside me. I let you fuck the sweetest piece in the whole camp, and you didn't really want to? So why'd you do it?"

"Because you dragged me into it."

"You're not answering my question. Why did you do it because I dragged you?"

"I don't follow."

"That tree over there. It won't fall down if I push it. Maybe another tree would. So I can't say: that tree fell because I pushed it. It has to be ready to fall. I dragged you into it, okay, but weren't you there to be dragged? You did it, so you wanted to."

Egon didn't know what to say. Axel was right. If any raping had gone on, then he'd done it, too.

"That packet you handed me at the Kopper. You remember that?"

"When they raided the place?" Axel laughed. "Sure, I remember."

"What was in it?"

"A controlled substance."

"Like what? Uranium?"

Axel glanced around. "LSD," he said.

"That was a shitty thing to do. You had no right to do that."

"You're right, it was pretty stupid of you to take it. But thanks. So why did you do it?"

"It was like I had to."

"So you had to," Axel said. "That's the whole secret: to make people want what you want them to want. Intimidation. Acting like you're running the show. Letting the other person think they'd be crazy not to. People are lazy; they'd rather obey than have to think up something to want. They're grateful when you think of something for them. Come on, out of the trenches, get yourselves mowed down. Yes sir, major. Come on, let's fuck! Fuck? Oh. Yeah, fuck. Great! And later, when they realize they didn't really want to . . . they've already got a bullet in them. Or a baby. And I'm supposed to feel guilty about that?"

"All you think about is yourself."

"Who else is there?"

Other customers had arrived, but Axel was being dragged along by the force of his argument, louder now, not caring who could hear. "If we waited for women to come up with the idea, mankind would have died out long ago. They don't want to; that's Nature. All that trouble—being pregnant, giving birth, getting stuck with a kid—who can blame them? But we have to make sure the seed gets where it belongs; we have to make them believe they want to. I'm good at that, sure. I help people make their mistakes, but they make them themselves. I do mankind a favor, and what does my best friend do? He calls me a rapist."

"So what do you really do for a living?" Egon asked. His own boldness took his breath away. It was because of that "best friend."

Axel wavered for a moment, then burst out laughing. "I'm in business," he said.

"What kind of business?"

"Jesus Christ, Egon. Powdered sugar."

"Powdered sugar? You mean heroin?"

"Heroin's brown," Axel said.

But Egon could tell it had been a slip of the tongue. Axel really did deal heroin, and he'd accidentally let on with that powdered sugar. They looked at each other and started laughing, roaring with laughter, a laugh with no hidden meaning or scorn, one you'd never pull out of, the laugh of two friends, two guys who had once screwed two girls in the same tent. That would always be there, and suddenly Egon hoped he was the only one who had that with Axel. The people at the other tables were watching, and some of them, the proprietress too, started laughing along with them.

Axel was the first to get serious. "Stars explode for me too sometimes," he said. "But not with women. It's when I fight. When I win, and the other guy becomes my fool."

"And now you're my fool," Egon said.

"I did a little time once," Axel said. "Three months. It was interesting. When I went in I didn't know what to expect. But after a week there was only one thing I didn't know: whether three months would be enough to make *everyone* my fool. But it was. From the purse snatcher to the warden. They all wanted what I wanted them to want. You don't know what life's about, Egon. It's taking everything you can take. Never ask for anything; that only makes people think of not giving it. Never be afraid. Fear is a waste of intelligence. Take. The chickenshits take a little; it takes guts to take a lot. That's the law of life. The law in the lawbooks is veneer."

"So you think I'm a chickenshit."

"You live in a different world."

"So tell me, chickenshit," Egon said. "Why did you come up to me, back then, at Central Station?" But even as he asked, he knew: Axel had chosen him as an admirer. They were the same age—in him, Axel had recognized a delegate from the world of the chickenshits, a touchstone for his daring.

But Egon's question had a surprising effect. Axel was quiet for a bit, then said: "I can't go back." It sounded heavy, melodramatic. "Maybe I envy you. But when I found out what I was, it was something you can't go back on. Goddamn it, Egon, you hear this crap? This is the kind of crap you spout when you're drunk. And I haven't touched a drop! *Madame!*"

He ordered another bottle of wine, and when that one and the next one were empty and darkness was falling, he said: "Come on, we're going to the whores. I know a good cathouse close to here. Someday, when they ask you what that Axel van de Graaf was really like, you should be able to say: he always came up with the sweet babes!"


TEN YEARS AFTER he'd started his studies, Egon went back to the Andes for the last time, to complete his doctoral research. He'd never spent more than two weeks there, but this time he stayed for three months.

After he finished his work he did what he'd been wanting to do all those years: he bought an old pickup in Quito and spent two months driving around Ecuador, Peru, Chile, and Bolivia. He climbed volcanoes, swam in lakes, hiked old Inca trails. On the afternoon of the last day he sold his car in Quito for a little less than he'd paid for it. His flight was leaving that night, and before dinner he took a walk in a park and drank a cup of coffee at a little pavilion. It was the end of an era. Exactly half his life ago he'd decided to become a geologist, and now he was one. The cup of coffee was his champagne. Maybe he'd never come back here again.

He tried to take in everything around him, the families walking by, the children playing ball in the grass, the shoeshine boy at the café's edge, because they shared this moment with him. But it didn't work; at a table across from him were three women, one of whom he knew at a glance he would still remember thirty years later. She had dark hair, round, vulnerable cheeks, and a subdued look that occasionally produced a free and cheerful laugh.

She glanced up at him, too, it seemed.

Imagine, he thought, that it's really this perfect. At the very moment my work is finished, I meet my wife. And before the shoeshine could switch to the other foot, Egon saw it all before him: how he would get up, walk over to the woman, go home with her to Buenos Aires, marry her, and have children—and come back here with her to find the shoeshine and show him those children.

Why not? he thought, and went over to them. They were from Holland; they'd been trekking around just like him. They were going home on the same flight that night. Her name was Adriënne. The four of them had dinner at a restaurant, and as they walked to the corner to catch a taxi to the airport, she took his arm.

They sat next to each other on the plane. When the lights went out they drifted in and out of sleep, and whenever he woke and saw her he thought: the first night we meet, we sleep together. He knew she was thinking that, too.

Adriënne lived in Amsterdam, her two friends were from Utrecht. The others took a train from Schiphol; Adriënne and Egon caught a taxi into town. For the second evening in a row they had dinner together at a restaurant, and again they spent the night together, this time in her bed. The next day, after they'd made love till almost noon, Egon discovered they had a common acquaintance: Axel van de Graaf. And, when he persisted, that she'd gone to bed with him once.

———

FOURTEEN YEARS LATER, when he and Adriënne split up, Egon knew they'd had only a few unspoiled hours together—from the little park in Quito to the discovery that she knew Axel.

It had happened once, at the Grim—Adriënne was one of those girls Axel had taken up to his room for a quickie. She couldn't remember exactly when, but it was back when Egon went there too. He might have seen her—maybe she was even one of the girls who'd created the thought in him: Axel fucks the girls from the party in his room.

He racked his brains, examined old photos of Adriënne, watched how she danced, how she stood with a glass in her hand, hoping to recall how she'd been that time at the Grim, how she'd come back down with Axel—but it was no use.

She'd hardly known Axel. Before that evening she'd run into him a few times at a café, had heard about his reputation. The fucking had been funny, an outrageously reckless thing to do. Just letting yourself be screwed right in the middle of a party, complete idiocy. She'd probably done it only so she could brag about it. Afterwards she'd burst out laughing, and she still laughed every time Egon started in about it.

"But how did it go?"

"He said: come on upstairs."

"Were you dancing with him?"

"No."

"Just talking."

"I'd been dancing with someone else, and then he put his hand on my belly and said: come on. With that look in his eye."

"It was the look that did it."

"And that hand."

"But you did it so you could brag."

"I actually thought he was kind of cute."

"You thought he was cute?"

"Only kidding. I did it because it was so absolutely weird and crazy. I thought it was pretty daring of me. Besides, he was no good. The classic lousy lover."

"And what if I'd put my hand on your belly?"

"Then I wouldn't have done it."

"With me it would have been absolutely weird and crazy too."

"But I wouldn't have done it."

"Why not? What does he have that I don't?"

"Just that. You have so much that he doesn't. A nice wife, for example."

They carried on that conversation for fourteen years, in the car, at the table, in bed, on ski lifts, in airplanes, in restaurants. He hadn't asked Vera Lanaker about it back on the blueberry hill at La Roche, but Egon wasn't going to let this witness off the hook so easily. Adriënne had felt Axel's power; he had made her want what *he* wanted her to want: she should be able to say why a bastard got more out of people than someone who was kind.

But she didn't know. "Because there's something exciting about him."

"Something exciting that I don't have."

"Yes, something exciting that you don't have. But not something exciting that makes him more worthwhile."

"Something sexy."

"That's the word I was looking for."

"You don't think I'm sexy."

"Dear, sweet Egon. I wish I'd never told you. It didn't mean a thing. And now I never want to hear another goddamn word about it."

But precisely because it didn't mean a thing, it meant everything. He had to pay with love for what Axel got with a gesture.

Axel had known Adriënne in a way he never would. She thought it had been "sort of funny"— but it was how evil triumphed over good!

ADRIËNNE'S FATHER had money. He owned a little chain of hotels in Holland and the south of Spain, and he bought a house for her and Egon in a nice part of Amsterdam. Once Adriënne had taken her economics degree, she went to work for him. After Egon received his doctorate, he was offered professorships at several small universities in America, but turned them down; Adriënne's job kept her in Amsterdam. He could teach two days a week at the university; until a full-time position came along, he took supplementary courses in geography and started working part-time at a high school on the outskirts of town.

One morning, as he was taking a little walk between classes, he suddenly got a smack on the shoulder. "Hey, Professor Doctor," a familiar voice said. "How's the caveman business?"

It was Axel.

He's been to bed with Adriënne, Egon thought.

"Come on, let's get a cup of coffee," Axel said. "Do some catching up."

Egon tried to remember how long it had been. The last time had been their trip to Belgium—eight or nine years ago. A lifetime. The boy of La Roche was gone for good now. Axel was fuller, calmer, but that was exactly what made him more menacing, or maybe it was the man he had with him, a giant with a coarse face and bristly blond hair, whose name was Bobby and who seemed to be his subordinate.

They came to a café on a quiet square with planters and benches, where people walked their dogs. Inside, Egon realized that Axel hadn't so much wanted to drink coffee with him; he'd taken him along to an appointment with some people he was going to meet anyway. At a large table by the window facing the square sat five or six men, leaning back in their chairs, tanned, laughing, chunky and muscular, with checkered shirts and suede jackets; men with the elegance of large, heavy animals.

Egon shook everyone's hand, saying, "Egon Wagter" each time, but they gave only their first names: Cor, Piet, Frans—all common names. The atmosphere was jovial, but Egon sensed they'd been waiting for a talk with Axel, which now, because of him, had to be postponed.

It took a while before Egon could figure out what these men reminded him of. An image from long ago loomed up in his mind—those two guys at the Grim, the ones who'd always stood so quietly to one side: Jan S., the people smuggler, and the other one, Faas. Hoodlums. And he saw how Axel fit in. He'd become a stereotype—no longer just himself, not like he'd been before.

Axel told the men that he and Egon had met at a vacation camp in the Ardennes when they were fourteen.

"Vacation, we never get around to that," one of them said, and they all laughed.

"Egon's a professor of geology," Axel said.

"Not yet," Egon said. "I'm a geography teacher."

"Don't ruin it," Axel said, sounding slightly irritated, and Egon realized he had actually wanted to shock the men with his friend's dumb profession.

"I'm trying to show you off," Axel said. "My friend Egon is an educated man."

"But not too smart, not if he hangs around with you," said Piet, or Cor. Laughter. It was actually more like giggling, but deeper and heavier.

I don't hang around with him at all, Egon thought.

"He's got his doctorate," Axel said.

"What's a learned guy like you know that we don't?" one of the men said.

"I know quite a lot about magmatic intrusions in tectonic processes," Egon said. He sensed that it sounded hostile.

"Can you make money with that?" One of the men had blurted it out in honest amazement, and now he was being laughed at a little.

"I write for professional journals," Egon said. "And I earn my living as a teacher. The satisfaction isn't in . . ." but he suddenly realized that any explanation of what moved him would be out of place. "Eighty thousand," he said.

"Eighty, not bad."

"A week, I take it?" another one said.

Once again that fat, self-important laughter that said: loser.

Egon looked around the circle. Cronies, he thought. These are cronies. He wondered what brought them together, what they'd talk about once he got lost. The idea that he was letting Axel show him off here irritated him, and feeling protected by him he said: "So what brings you together?"

The laughter that followed was truly roaring, but there was no gaiety in it. Axel laughed too, with the long, inhaling gasps Egon remembered from La Roche. This was how kings would laugh at a savage who'd done something for which others would be hanged.

"We work out together a lot," someone said.

When the laughter had died down again, Axel pulled him into a conversation, just between the two of them. He was doing all right. After that one time he'd never gone to prison again, but he clearly didn't like talking about himself. He asked Egon about his life, and Egon told him about his slim chances of finding a professorship, and about Adriënne. He saw there was no recognition at the name, and didn't say there could be.

"And what about you, have you finally relaxed a bit with women?" he asked, hating himself for the shyness behind that ridiculous way of putting it.

"I relax every day with women," Axel said.

When Egon said he had to get back to school, Axel laid a hand on his sleeve and gave him a look he probably thought expressed eternal friendship.

"Hey," he said. "If you ever get into trouble, come to me. I'm always there for my friends."

On the street, Egon realized these must have been underworld figures he'd been drinking coffee with. That Bobby was a bodyguard, of course. He'd sensed it the moment they went into the café, but dared to know it only now. Eighty thousand a week, that probably wasn't even a joke; they probably made that kind of money. Four million a year, could be. He'd been sitting there with millionaires. And they'd probably all been carrying pistols. Axel, too. It saddened Egon to think that people busied themselves with that kind of posturing, with pistols and bodyguards, with their millions and their scorn for a law-abiding citizen like himself. But at the same time you had to respect the brains and strength it took to learn the laws of that world, and hold your own in it. That's what Axel had wanted to show him, that those other guys just had to wait—only then did it dawn on Egon what that cup of coffee had really meant: Axel could *make* them wait. He hadn't just wanted to show him his world; but also that he was on top of it.

———

THREE DAYS LATER, all the front pages carried stories of a shoot-out at a boathouse in Loosdrecht: one man killed and two badly wounded. One of the wounded, the "former fraternity man Axel v.d. G. (34)," was thought to have fired the deadly shots. The other wounded man's name was Albert S.; the dead man was Pietje de Neve. It had probably been a showdown between drug barons.

So he *had* been carrying a pistol, Egon thought. A boy he'd seen sent out to pick blueberries, who'd walked along bellowing about ninety-nine bottles of beer on the wall. Egon wondered whether the gathering in the café had had something to do with it, if Albert and Pietje had been among the Cors and Piets he'd seen there. Maybe he had been the last person to make Pietje laugh.

Axel himself was at death's door. Egon hoped he'd die, if only for having the bad taste to be struck by bullets.

The papers were full of stories about the former fraternity brother, son of a hospital director from Hilversum, who was now a heavyweight in the drug world, drove a Rolls-Royce, had millions. Axel had been drawn into an ambush. He'd known that, but he had gone anyway. Without his bodyguard. Double or nothing, dead or feared like death. It was brave, but that bravery filled Egon with aversion—exactly the way it had, he realized now, the first time he'd seen Axel. It was pitiful to win admiration by playing with your life, whether you climbed a scaffolding or walked into a boathouse where men with guns were waiting for you. Axel's bravery was stupidity, a lack of self-respect. He'd become a caricature, with his Cors and Pietjes, his Bobby, his sweet babes, his Rolls-Royce, the bullets in his body, his struggle with death in a heavily guarded hospital.

For twenty years Egon had looked up to him; now he knew that had been a mistake—*he* was the winner. Axel was right, the law *was* veneer, a figment without roots in reality, but true strength was shown precisely by obeying it anyway, and by creating something of value within those bounds. While Axel had spread pestilence with his drugs, had killed a man, had restlessly filled cunt after cunt, Egon had added something to the knowledge of the world—something small, but something worthwhile. He and Adriënne had their eye on a little house in France, had started thinking about having a child. What they'd said around the campfire at La Roche had come true: he was a geologist, and Axel had wasted his life. He was going to die, or spend years in jail.

AXEL SURVIVED, and about six months later, after he'd had time to recover from his wounds, the trial was held. Egon went, and saw lots of familiar faces in the gallery: Bobby the giant, another two or three men he'd seen in the café, the old Grimmy Bear René, and, in the press section, Michiel Polak, the journalist he'd talked to sometimes at the Grim, the one who'd written that bit about the people smuggling.

When Axel was brought in, Egon saw that he was limping. A woman in one of the front benches suddenly stood up, and she and Axel hugged each other briefly. The guards seemed to let them. Axel looked around for people he knew in the gallery and nodded a few times—brief, friendly nods—but when he saw Egon his face creased into a surprised, happy smile.

During the proceedings, Egon saw from the reactions in the gallery that Axel's supporters and those of the dead Pietje formed two camps, on either side of the aisle, and that without realizing it he had sat on Axel's side. But most of all he felt the bond between the two groups. It went deeper than the murder that separated them for the moment; they were one front across from the fresh-faced, dressed-up citizens at the table, whose rules versus the real law, that of the criminals, were as ridiculous as a weather forecast versus the weather. The snickering at the naïveté of the judge, when he acted surprised that a person would take his pistol along for a workout, was unanimous.

One after another the witnesses perjured themselves blandly, about loads of hash they knew nothing about, ships they didn't own, weapons that had accidentally ended up in their pockets. They were salespeople, fitness-club owners, mechanics, café proprietors; there was not a brothel keeper, not a bodyguard, not a drug runner among them. They were so hollow, it was a wonder the bullets didn't pass right through them. Albert Spralinks, the wounded pal of Pietje de Neve, was apparently known in his own circles as "The Comb." They all had nicknames like that, maybe to increase the fear they spread, just like the men in the café. Egon wondered how many murders they accounted for among them, ultimately including their own. And in the midst of all this violent falsehood, Axel seemed utterly at ease, as if it were just part of the job to sit in courtrooms like this and let the whole farce roll over you.

The atmosphere was so routine that Egon was shocked when the prosecutor demanded nine years.

Nine years!

Axel nodded, and was led away.

EGON LEFT the courthouse, depressed. He had to think before he knew why—it was that woman. He would have expected a slut, something consisting entirely of lipstick and tits, but this was a nice person, with refined gestures, not ridiculously young, a woman he would have looked at himself. She knew the world Axel moved in and she seemed to accept it. Egon had turned down an expedition to Surinam and Brazil because he didn't want to leave Adriënne alone for four months; this woman would wait years for Axel to get out of prison.

THE ASSISTANT PROFESSORSHIP Egon had hoped for for so long went to someone else. It was a disappointment, but he continued to contribute book reviews to the journals; he wrote a school brochure about geology with a colleague; he took on more hours at his school. Although he was now teaching things he would have liked to discover himself to people who weren't interested, it was still satisfying that his school, since he'd been there, had produced more geology students than ever.

One day Adriënne asked him if he'd like to join her father's company as coordinator for his Spanish hotels. His Spanish was perfect, he already knew her father's company; he would earn twice what he did now—it could become their family enterprise.

Egon had seen the question coming for years, and had played out the conversation that would follow many times in his mind.

"Do you love me?" he asked.

"Yes."

"You love Egon Wagter?"

"Yes?"

"Then you don't want me to do it. Because then I wouldn't be Egon Wagter anymore. Egon Wagter is a geologist. Someone who felt a passion when he was young that became part of him, a part of him you can't take away without making him something he

isn't. Whether he's a good geologist, whether he's successful—
that doesn't matter. It is what he is. If you want to love Egon
Wagter, you have to accept that, too, even if he's only a geography
teacher who gives grades that don't matter, even if he has added
only one little grain of sand to the knowledge of the earth."

"Think about it," Adriënne said.


AXEL'S SENTENCE melted away like snow in the sun. He got six
years, took it to a higher court, heard four years demanded there,
finally got three, and, a few months after that verdict, he was
released early on good behavior. If you didn't count the time he'd
had to stay in the hospital anyway, killing that man had cost him
less than eighteen months.

The shoot-out had made him famous. Not just because of his
background, but also because he was said to be an innovator in
Dutch crime, with an organization that spanned ten countries or
more, through which hundreds of millions of guilders flowed,
and which acted with extreme violence. In his newspaper, Michiel
Polak ascribed a whole series of liquidations to him. Axel took
him to court, and lost.

Even if only a quarter of what was said was true, Egon read in
horror about the cornering of rackets, intimidation, fines, sawed-
off legs, and chopped-off dicks—the world of unwritten laws and
unwritten punishments, the hell over which Axel was now a king.

Of all the atrocities, one story shocked Egon most: that of the
first liquidation Axel was said to have ordered, years ago. Two
men had strolled into a busy restaurant and shot someone dead
while he was eating. Egon remembered it; back then that kind of
thing had been new in Holland, it had been big news in all the
papers. The gunmen had never been caught. In his old pocket

diaries he checked when Axel had driven him around Belgium—
two weeks after that killing.

It was chilling, unbelievable: the young man who had sat in
that lovely garden at Hurennes, holding forth on the relations
between men and women, to whom he had explained how stars
exploded when you held hands with a girl—who had fished for the
address of someone who had butted in on him while he was making it—in whom you could almost still see the naughty saltshaker-
climber of the Davy camp—that young man had already said to
one of his flunkies: "Blow away what's-his-name for me."

AFTER LOSING his suit against Polak, Axel let the papers and
magazines do as they pleased. He made no effort to be invisible;
on the contrary, he became more visible all the time. He'd never
cared about clothes, but now he used that to create his persona.
In a childish reversal of his wealth, he could be seen walking
through the city unshaven, in worn-out tennis shoes and a drab
raincoat—a king's robe displaying that very wealth, along with
the loneliness that goes with kings. Surrounded by a few bodyguards in expensive suits, to be sure. He still limped, which
only increased his fearsome mystique. A shiver ran through you
when you saw that deadly scarecrow. Everyone knew him—for
the general public, he was the only murderer you could see in
real life.

A few times, Egon saw him, too. He would have liked to have
sentimental thoughts at those moments, to think about the inno-
cence of the boy of La Roche that had been lost now. But Axel had
been a bastard even then. Whenever Egon saw him, he would
duck into a side street or a shop. But one time, while he was eat-

ing a snack at a sandwich shop, he felt a hand on his shoulder, and when he looked around he saw Axel's burning blue eyes.

"What was in the saltshakers?" Axel asked.

"Nothing," Egon said.

"Nothing," Axel nodded. "We're doing all right, eh, guy? Let's keep it that way." And he walked on, stared after by everyone in the shop until he was out of sight and Egon felt the lingering awe focus on him.

Someone like that will be on the front page someday, he thought, slumping out of a car with his mouth open, riddled with bullets. But it didn't happen. A wedding photo of Axel appeared in the paper, with that nice woman from the courtroom. Her name was Iemy. They had children, they lived in the most expensive part of town, and Axel kept walking around in his millionaire's rags, undisturbed and unhindered. One time a car exploded that he might have gotten into, Bobby the bodyguard was killed, but nothing happened to Axel. He visited galleries, bought paintings, had a boat take part in a big sailing race. In Ratanakiri, a Dutch businessman, Herbert Doornenbosch, was arrested with a couple of kilos of heroin in the false bottom of his suitcase. There was mention of the death penalty, and of the possible involvement of Axel van de Graaf. And Axel sat on a bench in the park and watched his daughter feed the ducks.

ONE DAY Adriënne came into Egon's study.

"We need to talk," she said, and she sat down on the old couch covered with notes and books, and exams he still had to correct. "What do you think of our relationship?"

DOORNENBOSCH WAS sentenced to death, appealed, and was sentenced to death again. He announced that he would not seek a pardon.

Egon bought a little apartment in the suburbs and applied for full-time teaching jobs. But geography was an elective these days, and he was too old for the oil companies now. The principal at his school suggested that he start teaching Spanish as well—getting the certificate would be no problem for him. Egon refused; he was a geologist.

In a newspaper he read that a team of American archaeologists, anthropologists, and biologists would be going to the Roraima shield in northeastern Brazil, close to Venezuela and Guyana, one of the remotest places on Earth. Roraima!—with almost the same sudden force he'd felt when he first knew he wanted to become a geologist, he knew he wanted to be a part of that expedition. He had read about Roraima in his very first geology book; it was one of the earth's oldest formations, maybe a billion years old. There might be a Window there, like the one at Hurennes. It made his head spin to think what a Window like that could show. It would be a hole in time, like all geological Windows—but a hole in a past that was a billion years old itself!

The article said nothing about geologists going along, and he wrote to the Americans right away. The reply was prompt; for forty thousand guilders, he could join them.

The bank refused to refinance his mortgage, and the publications he approached weren't interested. He kept hearing what Axel had said to him at that sandwich shop: "We're doing all right, eh guy?" What he had meant was: I'm doing fine, and you're a loser. That was his role in Axel's life, as established back on the platform at Central Station: he was the witness to Axel's triumphs, the proof that Axel was right.

Axel had fucked everything that moved, and undoubtedly still did, and he had an Iemy who posed smiling with him and the children. Egon had spent fourteen years with Adriënne, Axel one minute, and right up to the end that one time at the Grim had been something exciting to her, something to think back on with pleasure. Egon had served science; Axel had served himself. Egon had never hurt a soul; Axel had driven counselors to despair, killed people, created junkies, helped Doornenbosch to the guillotine. He was a celebrity, filthy rich, while Egon didn't even have the few thousand guilders he needed to make the dream trip of his youth.

All you had to do was be a bastard and the world lay at your feet. Axel was right, civilization was veneer, an alliance of the chickenshits to protect themselves against the true rulers, those who took what they wanted.

There was only one law: Axel's law.

I admit it, Egon thought. I lose. He wins.

EGON FIGURED it out. The heroin Doornenbosch had with him had been worth about five million—how much would the courier get who smuggled something like that? One percent was already fifty thousand guilders—that must be about it. And even if it was a little less, it would be enough to go with the Americans. He thought back on Friso and Hildegonde, the adventure Axel had offered him then, his regret at letting it pass. This was a little different, a guillotine awaited you here, but that's exactly what made it dazzling: to die or to be a geologist!

A date was fixed for Doornenbosch's execution. Egon felt the man's fear, his loneliness in that cell, far from everything he knew and loved—but he also felt the glee Doornenbosch must have felt when he'd stopped being good, the delight in his daring as he'd walked around Ratanak, his deadly charge with him, the reckless-ness of it all—like that of an Adriënne going upstairs with Axel.

Imagine: in Ratanakiri.

That alone!

## 3. Oum Phen

THE DISCOVERY OF the bodies of two Westerners in a parking lot near the airport at Ratanak, the capital of Ratanakiri, led among other things to the presence, two weeks later, of a Dutch journalist at the other end of town, in the Russei Keo district, where fish were raised in big ponds.

The ponds were bordered by low dikes of brown earth on which little palm trees grew, and behind the idyllic green of the mango trees along the banks you would almost have expected the villas of millionaires. Yet in Russei Keo whole families lived together in raised huts the size of beach cabanas. Beside them were little ditches through which you saw the occasional inhabitant wade, trousers or sarong hitched up, and before each hut stood a big earthen pot for rainwater. The thought of running water, gas, electricity, happiness would be absurd here.

Walking in front of Michiel Polak, the journalist, was George Mijnsherenland, first secretary to the Dutch embassy in Ratanak,

a dapper fellow who looked twenty-three but could just as easily have been forty. A fairy, no doubt, but a good fellow.
Polak grinned inwardly at Mijnsherenland's tireless verve, the
part in his hair, the crease in the trousers of his impeccable tropi-
cal suit.

It was seven o'clock in the morning.

The odor of fish, an elemental thing after three paces, hung
over the ponds like an atmosphere of its own. Here all was fish.
Little fish hung out on lines to dry, lay on flats, in pails, wrinkled
together in a huge tub like some massive brain. At one corner of a
pond glistened the silver of a million suffocated fish, and on the
dikes sat families coated with fish slime, cleaning fish on chopping
blocks, hacking off heads, pulling out intestines. Babies and little
children played on the ground, some wearing only pants, others
just T-shirts, the little girls with colorful earrings and bead neck-
laces. Two boys were toting huge plastic bags full of cans; children shot at each other with bamboo slingshots. Russei Keo
brimmed over with life, almost as if there weren't enough people
and fish to divide it among.

In the middle of a pond, a boy, only his bare chest sticking out
of the water, was stepping laboriously, slowly, bent over like he
was walking into a gale.

"Pulling in the nets," George said. "Gets him three cents
a kilo."

"Dutch cents?"

"Come on. Dollar cents. You don't think these people would
let themselves be exploited, do you? General Suffering wouldn't
like that." Mijnsherenland referred to General Sophal as General
Suffering so consistently that Polak had stopped hearing it as a
joke and had started thinking of the dreaded ruler by that name
himself.

Somewhere here, amid the people and the fish of Russei Keo, was the home of Oum Phen, the boy who was waiting, in the same cell complex where Herbert Doornenbosch had waited, to be beheaded—when the sun rose again, he would be executed for the twin slaying in the parking lot.

They were looking for his mother.

George, who had been in Ratanak for two years and spoke Ratan well, occasionally asked directions. Amid the hard, undecipherable sounds Polak recognized the name Oum Phen, and was shocked that someone with a name like that was going to have his head cut off. Herbert Doornenbosch, that was something else; that was a name you could die like a dog with, but Oum Phen . . . That was a name for a doll that belonged to a cute child.

The fishpond dwellers had a way of staring morosely, sullenly into space, but whenever George spoke to one of them a shy smile would appear. Sometimes Polak thought he saw recognition and dismay when Oum Phen's name was mentioned—one boy slid his hand across his throat, to the cheerful laughter of his comrades—but there was no sign that the people of Russei Keo resented the two of them, oppressors, imperialists who earned more in a single breath than they would earn in a lifetime—even though one of their own was going to get killed at first light, because he had no longer been able to bear the wealth of people like them. The families working at their fish-chopping blocks on the dikes moved aside readily when Mijnsherenland and Polak came along, missing out on a few costly tenths of a cent just to let the men pass. That Oum Phen might be innocent probably never occurred to them. Maybe they wouldn't even care. Injustice could kill you slowly, or it could be swift.

A man came wading toward them down one of the side ditches, hunched over, his feet groping along the invisible bottom, a filthy rag knotted around the stump of a severed arm. "Doctor's orders," George said. "Walk through plenty of dirty water. Before you know it, you'll be fit as a fiddle!"

It was the dry season. During the rainy season there were no dikes and ponds here, just one huge pond, with only the raised huts sticking out of the water. George laughed at Polak's idea that people would get around in boats then. Boats were for the rich few; the others waded, just like they did now, only the water was deeper. Pizza boys had to swim.

They arrived at a hut that leaned crookedly against a larger one. A girl was treading about in a tub full of slime, an intact fish head visible here and there.

"*Prahok*," George nodded. "Fish pulp, mmm."

The girl was carrying a baby in a cloth slung around her neck; an older child was playing on the ground with a bottomless pail. When George spoke to her, the young woman stepped out of the tub and walked to the opening of the little hut. They had found Oum Phen's house. This was where he had lived until he was taken away, two weeks ago. George dropped to his haunches and peered inside. Polak tried to look over his shoulder. In the darkness of the hut, a woman was squatting. He saw a little stool, plates, a broken green flip-flop.

Six-by-six, he figured.

The woman crawled outside: Oum Phen's mother. The light made her blink. Her hair was black on the sides, gray on top. Her face was pretty.

George told her what Polak had come to do, and she nodded.

"Well, this is Mrs. Oum," George said. "Fire away."

In the woman's eyes Polak saw only dignity. Or rather, he saw nothing. The mother of a condemned man in the final hours of his life—how easy to read bitterness, raging sorrow, despair into any stare. But with her unfathomable Ratanakirian gaze, she looked just like everyone else here. And even if he did think he saw some emotion, maybe her emotions were as unlike his as the languages they spoke. Polak wondered whether she saw through him. He wasn't here because he gave a damn about her son, or about her, but because the mother of a condemned man made good copy.

Before long an audience had gathered, a bit giggly but still respectful and quiet, the children too. Someone brought over a little bench for Mijnsherenland and Polak to sit on. Polak put his bag on the ground, but a woman hurried over and slid a piece of cardboard under it.

"How many people live here?" he asked.

"Seven," George translated.

"Who are they?"

"My daughter and her husband. They have four children. She doesn't mention herself," George said. "Always funny, that."

"And she doesn't mention Oum Phen."

"True, but then he doesn't live here anymore."

Polak thought he detected a sparkle of pride in the woman's eyes when Oum Phen was mentioned—the only one in the family who'd risen above the fish-filled atmosphere. Even if he'd only made it to death row. Because of him, Westerners had come to Russei Keo, to her house.

"What was she doing when we got here?"

"She was making a bracelet for the child."

His questions and her answers didn't matter. He already had everything he needed: the fish heads between the daughter's toes, the piece of cardboard, the crease in Mijnsherenland's trousers.

"Is Oum Phen a nice boy?" he asked.

"Yes."

"Where is Oum Phen's father?"

"Dead. In the war."

"How old is Oum Phen?"

The woman thought about it. "He's past twenty," she said, sounding doubtful. "Good question," George said. "Telling, isn't it? She's not exactly sure. Even though it's been in the paper."

"How old is she?"

"She was born in the Year of the Monkey, before the French left. We'll look that one up when we get back. You can bet she's younger than you are."

"What kind of work did Oum Phen do?"

"He watches cars and opens doors. She means he's a beggar. He's handicapped. He has only one leg."

"Did he like his job?"

"She doesn't understand the question."

"Did he do his work with pleasure?"

"*Tas,*" the woman nodded.

George said, "I think she means: he was glad to have a job at all. Well, a job. To earn some money."

"What were his hobbies?"

"Playing with model trains and tennis. Try asking questions that make sense."

"Has she ever received a letter? I mean, does the postman ever come here? That just popped into my mind. Sorry, you're confusing me."

"She has never received a letter."

"Can she read?"

"Yes. But no one writes to her. Sad, isn't it?"

"Egon Wagter, does she know that name?" George tried pronouncing it in different ways, but Polak saw no recognition.

"Does she know that Oum Phen has been in the paper in Holland?"

The woman nodded. "Holland is where the Dutch people came from."

"Has she visited Oum Phen in prison?"

The woman was silent and spoke only after a moment.

"He is being treated well," George said.

"But has she been there? Has she seen that herself?"

"No."

"Has she said goodbye to him? Is she going to say goodbye to him?"

"No. No money. Too far to walk."

"Does she believe that Oum Phen murdered them?" Now Polak did see a change in the woman. She knew her son was innocent. With far less reason that he had, but with far greater force.

She said nothing. Oum Phen's sister said something.

"His sister says: General Suffering is very good for the country," George said.

"Fair enough."

"Yes, they're definitely shitting bricks."

"Do they have a picture of Oum Phen?" Polak asked. To his surprise, the woman nodded. She crawled into the crib and came back out with a little picture frame, which she handed to Mijnsherenland. There was a color picture in it. For George, too, it was the first time he'd seen Oum Phen. He had a rather pudgy face, a little straw hat that seemed to perch loosely on his head, a girlish moustache. Something startled about his eyes. A brown sports shirt with a white collar.

"Are they going to do anything special to mark his execution?" Polak asked.

The woman shook her head briskly. "Scared to death," George said.

Polak asked if he could take a picture, and with a horrifying gesture Oum Phen's mother straightened her hair, her blouse. He took a couple of pictures, then asked if Oum Phen's sister would join her mother. She tried to duck away, but the people around began laughing and pushing, as though she'd be mad not to seize an opportunity like this. Finally she picked up her oldest child and stood next to her mother. Polak asked the mother to hold up her picture of Oum Phen, and he took a few like that, too, then a couple of close-ups of the little portrait.

It was time to go.

He asked George if he could give them some money.

"Sure. How much were you thinking of?"

"I don't know. A hundred dollars?"

George looked at him as if he was out of his mind.

"A hundred dollars, do you have any idea how much that is? They'd have to drive a scooter-taxi six times around the world to earn that. You want her to join junior on the chopping block? Make it one dollar. That's more dollars than she's ever seen in one place before."

Polak opened his wallet to give her whatever small bills he had—and realized the blunder he'd almost made. He'd been about to hand her a twenty—a bill like the one that had sealed her son's fate. Before he could find anything else, George plucked the wallet out of his hand and gave the woman a dollar.

Oum Phen's mother and sister folded their hands and bowed, and George and Polak did, too. The mother said something. "She feels ashamed for the sorrow the Dutch people have to bear," George said.

While they were following the dikes back to where their driver was waiting, Polak asked himself what purpose there was in someone like Oum Phen, what the point was of his ever having lived—whether he had been anything more than a product of fucking, a fish among the fish.

IN THE EMBASSY CAR, while they were sitting wedged between scooter-trucks full of happy, waving children, the two-way radio crackled. George put on the headphones, carried on a brief conversation in Ratan, then looked at Polak with an expression that stopped Polak's blood.

"He'll do it," George said. "Nine o'clock on the dot, with General Suffering."

HE WOULD HAVE liked to go to him straightaway, stinking of his subjects, but Polak had let himself be dropped off at the Holiday Inn, had freshened up, and now he sat beside George in the backseat of the car that was taking them to the Presidential Palace. A nonsense drive: it was only three steps from the hotel. But tyrants were not to be visited on foot.

Even though General Suffering would be the first head of state he'd meet in person, Polak was ashamed of his dry throat. Mijnsherenland, for whom such meetings were all part of the job, and who had shaken General Suffering's hand twice before, was quiet too. After all, this wasn't some neat prime minister or well-bred monarch they'd be facing; this was a mass murderer. There could be no behavior that wasn't unworthy.

From the most outside sentry to the most interior of secretaries, the word seemed to be: treat the Dutch visitors as distinguished guests. They didn't have to show their papers; they weren't searched. People knew who they were. Five minutes after they'd reported to the gate, they were sitting in garden chairs in a sort of greenhouse, an air-conditioned, glassed-in-from-the-sky garden with gurgling fountains, a brook with fat goldfish, statues of gods and former rulers, and a bust of General Suffering in his favorite pose: eyes raised to view the Great Future of his country. Flag stands held two spread-out banners: one with the red, white, and green of Ratanakiri; the other with the national emblem, the temples at Ta Prohm, in red on a white field. A lizard scurried away, and a little man in a plain grayish-blue tunic came in, so casually that Polak could already see the line in his story about how, despite everything, a secretary or gardener could move about freely in a palace like this. With his small stature, his wrinkly bald head and big eyes, the little man was like a carica-ture of all those portraits of Sophal he'd seen around Ratanak— and Polak's breath jammed in his throat. It was Worker Number One, the Lord of Ratanakiri, ruler over life and death: General Sophal Eng Neang.

They stood and bowed, hands folded in front of their chests, as they had with Oum Phen's mother. George said something in Ratan in which Polak recognized his own name, and the general took Polak's hand and shook it. His hand was soft, but the gesture was brisk. He pulled a pack of Lucky Strikes out of his pocket, held it out to them, then lit one himself. He sat down and ges-tured to them to do the same.

Polak didn't smoke, but for a moment he felt he couldn't refuse. A cold sweat broke out.

General Suffering wafted away Mijnsherenland's Ratan; he spoke French. That, too, was a token of courtesy; he could have called in an interpreter. That he'd agreed to receive Polak at all was a gesture in itself: he seldom spoke to journalists. His French was beautiful, clipped, firmly articulated, as if he were reading his text from Polak's forehead. Between well-turned phrases he let silences fall, seemingly to make you feel that you were to be quiet even then.

That little man radiated power, the kind of power you also felt with Axel van de Graaf. Sophal was a man who dared to inflict harm, on a large scale. In the evil of that there was something grand, and to his horror Polak found himself admiring that. He wondered whether he'd dare to say what he had to say to justify his visit: in Holland, Oum Phen is believed to be innocent.

Sophal had come a long way. He may not have been a product of the fishy sludge like Oum Phen, but as a naked little boy he too had run around amid the garbage of Ratanak. At school a good intellect had manifested itself, and the king had sent him to France. In Paris he had studied highway engineering, listened to Sartre and Juliette Greco, published poems, been squeezed flat in the *métro*, and at a certain point he must have had a vision of the ennoblement of the Ratanakirian. He had helped the king to drive out the French, helped a rival to drive out the king, had driven out the rival, and, after that, had dared to leave all things human behind and exterminate everything that got in the way of his vision.

General Suffering hoped Polak had had a good trip, that his stay in Ratanak would be pleasant, that the honorable secretary of the embassy would deliver his humble compliments to the ambassador, and that he would find more interesting places to take his guest than ponds where fish were raised.

A murderer is warning me, Polak thought.

Mijnsherenland nodded.

The general trusted that Polak's article would provide a good picture of the modern, progressive Ratanakiri. He praised the beautiful and industrious Netherlands, saying that although the two countries were separated by half the globe, he hoped they would always be special friends. Two recent, unfortunate incidents—and Polak knew then that Sophal would manage to leave Doornenbosch, Wagter, and the woman unnamed—could do nothing to affect those ties. Ratanakiri had shown that it would not hesitate to severely punish foreign criminals who endangered the health of its young people, but also that his countrymen who harmed Ratanakiri's guests could count on equal severity.

Polak wondered whether General Suffering knew that his power, just like Oum Phen's mother's fear, made it impossible for him to speak plainly. To patch things up with his Dutch trading partners after the beheading of Doornenbosch, he had made Egon Wagter, who was clearly the same brand of smuggler, more or less a hero of the republic, and he was presenting Holland with the sacrifice of a real, live Ratanakirian. Ratanakirians enough. That the boy was innocent—a mere detail. It didn't occur to Sophal that Holland might find his gesture even more repellent than what he hoped it would patch up.

The police, General Suffering went on, had done fine detective work; the criminal Oum Phen had been promptly located, had confessed, had been condemned to death, and would receive his punishment this very night. "And you," he said, "shall attend his execution."

To Polak, it was like hearing the death sentence himself. He saw George recoil in his chair. And, in the same moment, he thought: what an opportunity.

Sophal had allowed his announcement to be followed by one of his silences, a silence that now forced Polak to speak.

"I knew Egon Wagter," he said.

He saw confusion in Sophal's eyes—maybe he didn't even know the name.

"You will see how his murderer pays," Sophal said. "You will tell your countrymen how he dies."

"In Holland, there is doubt as to Oum Phen's guilt," Polak said. The words were out of his mouth, it was as though he watched them go, on their way to their meaning. From the corner of his eye he saw George stiffen. "The Dutch are opposed to capital punishment," he added, immediately regretting the cowardice of that qualification. Now that he'd ruined it, he saw how lovely and clear his phrase had been, in the brief moment it had stood alone.

Polak then saw something in General Suffering that he would never have dreamed of seeing in such a man: disappointment. He had offered the people of Holland a gift, and Polak had said it wasn't nice, that he should have come up with a better murderer, one who was guilty.

"The criminal Oum Phen was defended by a very good lawyer," Sophal said, "and the judge who sentenced him studied at the Sorbonne."

Polak couldn't believe his ears. The Sorbonne! Didn't Sophal realize that a French head of state wouldn't brag about the Sorbonne, that his doing so meant that nothing had come of his vision—that he'd had all those people murdered for nothing?

Polak nodded. Of course, the Sorbonne. Then it must be all right.

He could be satisfied: he'd justified his visit to General Suffering, and it had produced a fantastic quote. Maybe Oum Phen wasn't even supposed to look guilty—maybe, in General Suffering's eyes, the atonement was all the greater with an innocent man condemned and the record speed with which he'd be executed, two weeks after the murders. And while Sophal's voice came to him from far away and Polak wondered if he would dare to witness the story of his life, he made the occasional scribble in his notebook. He thought of writing *bastard*, but didn't dare. He wrote: *jeunesse, amitié, victoire*—words he plucked from Sophal's speech as though it were a grab bag.

And then he looked at him again, a little seventy-year-old man, soft-spoken, with almost feminine gestures, and between two raised fingers a Lucky Strike from which smoke curled up majestically; his little wrinkled face stern and lonely, cut off forever from the possibility that the three of them would sit in a café, thumping each other on the back about the absurdity of it all.

THEY SAT in the embassy car without speaking. Polak was exhausted, as though he'd been holding back a boulder that would otherwise have crushed him. At one swoop, Sophal had taken his trip to Ratanakiri, his whole story, his memory of Egon Wagter, and reduced it all to the issue of whether or not he would go to Oum Phen's execution; would dare to go, or would dare not to go. He tried to imagine what it would be like, but he saw only himself and that boy, looking at each other. That made it seem as if it would go on forever, but of course it would be over before you knew which way to look.

"A penny for your thoughts," Mijnsherenland said.

"Unbelievable. They just picked somebody."

"Yes, rotten luck that. Are you going?"

"I don't know."

"Oum Phen will be going."

Polak realized it was his only chance to see him in real life.

MIJNSHERENLAND HAD already pointed out the Building of Friendship between Ratanakiri and Vietnam the evening before, when they had driven into town from the airport, but now Polak was really seeing it: a squat, stern rectangle, a good symbol for a friendship of Sophal's.

The chauffeur drove into the lot and parked at the entrance to the building.

A light breeze made the heat bearable; when they climbed out, Polak stretched. There weren't many cars. A lot of the building's windows were dead; there were brownish spots on the walls. Cigarette boxes and candy wrappers swirled around in a miniature whirlwind; a can tinkled over the macadam. The chain-link fence had a bright fringe of paper and other trash. Behind it a rocky field stretched to the road, with a crooked palm in the middle. On the other side, behind the building, were the movements and sounds of the airport.

Another car was just arriving, stopping at the fence. A girl in a blue skirt and a white blouse got out with a pile of folders in her arms and walked quickly to the building's entrance, trotting a few steps now and then, holding her hand on the papers to keep them from blowing away.

"Elite," George said. "Two hundred dollars a year."

"Is she keeping an eye on us?"

George laughed. "Of course not, that's his job." He laughed and nodded at the chauffeur, who nodded back amiably.

George walked over to the girl's car and stood there. "This is more or less where your friend's car was," he said. "And there was the woman's car." Suddenly he seemed to buckle over. "Christ," he said. "Look."

Polak walked over and saw a pale, brownish stripe on the ground. A trail, almost indistinguishable from the concrete, broken now and then, sometimes a pair of thin lines next to each other, then one thick one again. Matter that had been in Wagter's body, or in the woman's.

The trail ended at a large, darker spot, from which ran a thin, meandering spoor to the place where her car had stood. She and Wagter had been found together, but they must have been attacked separately at their own cars and then, fatally wounded, crawled to each other. Where that big spot was, their bodies had been found the next morning by the watchman, Monsieur Pouc. He was the one they had come here to meet.

George went into the building; Polak walked around and took pictures, including one of the chauffeur, who pointed laughingly at the big spot, gesturing as if he was gutting a cow. "Big blood," he said.

Polak looked at the trails and thought about that woman's children. The autopsy had shown that she'd had children, and that she was between thirty-five and forty years of age—they must be young children. Her identity was still a mystery, those children must be out of their minds with not knowing what he knew. And he'd give anything to know who *they* were.

For the time being, her body was interred at the International Hospital in Ratanak.

For a few days she had been Rosa Zinger, a Dutch woman. As Rosa Zinger she had rented her car, stayed at the Hotel Concorde, and was booked on the night flight to Athens that was to depart a couple of hours after she was murdered. But Rosa Zinger was alive and well; a forty-two-year-old secretarial temp in The Hague whose passport had been stolen a few months ago.

From a window a man looked out at Polak, probably envious that he could just walk around like that.

Suddenly it dawned on him that Ratanakiri's cynicism could be read right here on the ground. He hadn't seen it at first, because of the dramatic import of the trails of blood—the crawling together of those dying people. Those trails proved that one man couldn't have done it. Wagter and the woman had each been attacked at their own cars—by two different killers.

Oum Phen had never been here.

When he had read in the paper about the death of his old acquaintance Egon Wagter, Polak had called the embassy in Ratanak. He'd gotten George Mijnsherenland on the line, who'd told him that a culprit had already been arrested, a one-legged beggar who had followed Wagter from a disco to a parking lot where he had a date with a woman. Mijnsherenland had found it strange that an invalid could overpower two well-nourished Westerners, and that Wagter and that woman had agreed to meet at a parking lot like this one. A couple of days later, he called Polak back. There had been a story in the paper about a record heroin haul: two young men had been arrested with five kilos. He'd wondered right away whether it might have something to do with the twin slaying—whether this was the heroin Wagter was supposed to have passed to the woman at that parking lot, or the other way around. The men arrested were two poor slobs who could never have come near that much heroin, or the kind of money that went along with it. The family of one of the men had a little food stand along the road to the airport, close to the parking lot. When no further news appeared about the record haul, Mijnsherenland believed he understood. There'd been panic over the two dead Dutch people; so soon after Doornenbosch, they couldn't afford that. General Sophal had needed a scapegoat, and fast, and that's what the beggar had become. Oum Phen's guilt had already been reported in Holland when they realized that the real murderers had been arrested by accident. But by that time they were of no use to them anymore: the two men would have made drug smugglers of the Dutch tourists. They had probably been disposed of quietly.

George came back outside with a lopsided, shriveled little man with big horn-rimmed glasses: Monsieur Pouc. He actually spoke a few words of French, but with such a heavy accent that neither Polak nor George could understand a word.

But Pouc's gestures said it all. When he'd come to work on that morning, he had immediately seen two cars that didn't belong in the parking lot, had immediately realized something was wrong. One car here, one car there. Even though it was still half-dark, he'd seen the blood, too, this trail here, he'd followed it, and there, by that car, he'd found the bodies. At first he'd thought someone had dropped a huge sack, but then he had seen hands and realized it was a body lying there. One body, he'd thought at first—that's how slashed up and tangled together those two had been—but then he'd seen the heads, the torn-open stomachs, pools of blood, two horribly mutilated cadavers. His *r*'s became theatrical, his French a parody of General Suffering's, and Polak saw that people were standing at the windows of the building now, their faces full of oohs and aahs at the bodies that had lain there and were now lying there again, at the massacre taking place here once more. Monsieur Pouc became the murderer, Polak too saw the knife in his hand. Pouc jumped around, stabbed, screamed, groaned, became the victims as well. He rattled, the blood spattered everywhere, and George recoiled, as though afraid to be hit by the spatters. And when the victims lay at his feet, a broad smile settled over Monsieur Pouc's face, childlike and free, and it was as though from behind all the windows in the building a thundering cheer went up.

AT POLICE HEADQUARTERS, an old French colonial building along a broad lane of palms, an unpleasant surprise awaited. They were received, not by the inspector who'd led the investigation and with whom George had made an appointment, but by a General Chhouk Rin, the deputy minister of police, a young man whose mirrored sunglasses couldn't hide his fear of saying something wrong. A portrait of General Suffering hung above his head.

Resignedly, Polak listened to Chhouk Rin's story, told in quite decent English, of the prompt and efficient investigation of the twin slaying. Six o'clock: Monsieur Pouc finds the bodies. Ten past six: police arrive on the spot, judicial inquiry service. Conclusion: man, woman, robbery; no money, jewelry, or identification found on the bodies. Nevertheless, quarter past six: identities established through car rentals; Wagter Egon, Dutch nationality, age forty-three; Zinger Rosa, also Dutch nationality, age forty-two.

In his mind, Polak added: six-sixteen: General Suffering woken by a call. Panic, another dead Dutchman, two no less, probably drug runners. What to do? Make it robbery with murder, seize culprit, off with his head, Sophal had said, and had gone back to sleep.

Polak could see Oum Phen, with his wispy moustache and his straw hat. What would he be doing now? Would they tell him there would be spectators? Would he be startled to see the white man there? Perhaps he would think: a brother, and forget his fear for a moment.

But Polak had to pay attention; he had to get the cynicism right. Wagter, as the police had established right away, had been staying at the Holiday Inn. Alone. Then he must have gone to the disco at the Concorde; every man alone in Ratanak went there. With his passport, found in his room, the police went to the Concorde. They woke the beggars sleeping there. The beggars identified Wagter, and said that Oum Phen had forced himself on him and, when Wagter left, had followed him on a scooter he'd taken from one of them. They knew Oum Phen to be a liar, a thief, and a knife fighter, and said he lived in Russei Keo. Less than two hours after the bodies were found, Oum Phen had been arrested there, at his mother's house, a twenty-dollar bill still in his pocket. He had confessed right away.

It was completely bald-faced. Why would Oum Phen keep twenty dollars on him if he'd hidden the rest of the loot? And where was the rest of it? Could he have taken the scooter just like that—did those other beggars even have a scooter? Could he have ridden with that wooden leg? Could that scooter have kept up with Wagter's car? Why had he followed Wagter when it would have been natural to assume that he was simply returning to his hotel? How could he have taken on the sturdy Wagter, and a woman to boot?

They'd just grabbed the first poor bastard they could find.

But maybe you had to look at it differently. Maybe they had taken the realization of Oum Phen's dreams off his hands, and tomorrow morning Polak would see the Oum Phen that the great ruler of his country had made of him: a reckless gangster who sees his prey, hops on a fast motorbike, speeds through the Ratanakirian night, black hair blowing in the wind, shifting gears effortlessly with his wooden leg, who robs the two Western oppressors, kills them with a few sweeps of his blade, as dauntlessly as he would die now.

"Did they find the loot?" Polak asked.

"He refuses to tell us where it is."

"Doesn't say much for the torturing around here," George said to Polak out of the corner of his mouth.

Chhouk Rin smiled, uncertain.

"Why were Wagter Egon and the woman in the parking lot?" Polak asked.

Chhouk Rin gestured apologetically. "The Ratanakirian air is known for arousing desire."

"How did they meet? They didn't come to Ratanakiri together."

"There is a Ratanakirian proverb. The man and the woman who are destined to meet will make day and night come together. We don't know. We can't know everything! Perhaps they met at the Silver Pagoda, or at the Palace. All the tourists go there. A ticket stub was found among Wagter's possessions."

"And they agreed to meet again at the parking lot?"

"It is possible."

"Why not at one of their hotels?"

"Perhaps they did not want to be seen together. The woman was married. She wore a wedding ring. She was a mother."

"And on the way to their rendezvous, Wagter stopped in at the Concorde?"

Chhouk Rin held up his arms, hands spread.

"Perhaps he wanted to drink something. Have no doubt. We found her hair on the backseat of his car."

"Do you have any idea who she was?"

"No. She was traveling under a false name. She was probably Dutch."

"There are no missing women in Holland who match her description," Polak said. "Why did she use a false name if she was just a tourist?" He realized what he was doing. Wagter and the woman were not supposed to be drug smugglers. The false name made them that anyway. The real murderers, who had done that too, had been made to disappear.

"Perhaps she did not want her husband to trace her. Perhaps she was looking for love."

Chhouk Rin admitted that the trail went cold in Bangkok—she had arrived by way of Bangkok, but the authorities there could not, or would not, say where she'd come from.

"I shall show you what the criminal Oum Phen did to your countrymen," he said. He took a pile of photographs from his desk and handed them to Polak.

They were large black-and-white pictures, with a stamp in the bottom right corner and a number written in ink inside each stamp. They had white borders and had been printed at a soft, pretty exposure—the work of someone who loved his profession.

They seemed to be presented as suspensefully as possible, but maybe they were simply in the order in which they'd been taken. The first picture showed only a van from a distance, and two passenger cars parked at the fence. In one of the following pictures Polak recognized the trails of blood. Then, between the two cars, a shape became visible: the bodies. Not very clearly at first, but the photographer had approached step-by-step, as if he'd wanted to respect the intimacy of the two people lying there dead together.

And then you saw them. Wagter lay on his left side, his left arm outstretched, and on it lay the woman's head. She had her left arm around him, her hand behind his head. Their foreheads touched. They had their eyes open. There was no dread in their look.

Polak recognized Wagter. Even though his face was gray with death, there was also something fresh about it. The woman had a sweet face that reminded him of Wagter's ex-wife.

They looked young.

And then Polak saw the picture that he knew right away would always stay with him. At first he thought he saw fish. Yes, of course, Oum Phen, fish, he thought when he saw the coiling, glistening mass in between Wagter and the woman. Then he saw that it was their intestines. They'd come out of their stomachs, and lay so tangled together that you couldn't tell whose was what.

The minister gloated.

Close-ups of the intestinal mass followed, all printed with the same care.

"The Ratanakirian eye for detail," George said, but it sounded weakish.

When all the pictures had been shown, Chhouk Rin signed a piece of paper and handed it to Polak. "The execution of the criminal Oum Phen," he said, "will take place tomorrow morning at six o'clock in the prison at Tuol Ek. You will be picked up from your hotel at four."

Polak tucked the paper away; admit one free. This was the ticket stub Wagter should have had.


HE LAY on his bed. Mijnsherenland had wanted to go on to the Concorde, to the grave of the unknown drug courier at the hospital, but Polak was finished. He had a headache from the heat, the time difference, the lack of sleep, his cowardice with Sophal, the impossible decision that had been forced on him, from all those intestines and chopped-off heads, Pouc's *cadavres terri-blement mutilés*—the seething-over soup of life and death in Ratanak.

In people there were intestines, nine meters of them, carefully propped into their stomach by millions of years of evolution, but if you cut open those stomachs, they came out. It was as if he was hanging in the air above that parking lot, above those pictures, and could zoom in, zoom out, go up, circle around and see everything, but he kept returning to those intestines and those faces, the terrible embrace of those two people. Chhouk Rin could lie as much as he wanted, but this was true. They were lovers.

But that was impossible.

As a normal tourist in Ratanak, you could be robbed and murdered—but surely not if you knew one of the world's biggest drug barons personally. Not if you were murdered along with someone who was traveling under a false name. Not in a parking lot like that. But still, that's how it was. They were lovers—and drug couriers at the same time.

He saw Egon Wagter before him, as he'd known him half a lifetime ago. Polak had been a reporter with a prominent weekly then, the paper's youngest ever. His glory days. The news desk was down in the old center of town, and sometimes when he'd worked late on a piece and was walking home, he would pass a house on a little canal where the sidewalk was always covered with bikes, and music and noise came through an open door. He went in one night and wound up in the midst of a party; people were dancing, necking, and drinking, and the joints went round. It was a fraternity house, the Grim, but no one asked him a thing, not that first time, and not after that. He'd gone there regularly for a while. There were always nice women at those parties, and that had netted him a few brief affairs.

But Polak's memory of the Grim was swallowed up by his memory of the young Axel van de Graaf he'd seen there. Even then Axel had been someone who immediately drilled his way into your consciousness; an ugly, intense young man with riveting eyes, unsympathetic and irresistible at the same time. He laughed a lot, a laugh that didn't invite you to laugh along, and he had this amazing way with women, but he also derived a strange pleasure from driving them into your arms. And he dealt drugs. Polak had bought a chunk of hash from him once, and another time a few cubes of LSD; you knew you could go to him for speed and heroin as well. It was an exciting thought to have watched a champion take his first steps.

But Polak had made a name before Axel did. The Grim had given him his first cover story, about a ring of people smugglers who operated half in the underworld, half through the Grim, and who'd caused at least seven students to wind up behind bars in Eastern Europe. His editor had cut Axel's name and all overt references to the Grim out of the story, which Polak had sorely regretted, especially since he suspected that Axel was the real leader. Later, when Axel's star had risen, Polak regretted it even more. How often that story would have been quoted.

The only real reason he remembered Egon Wagter was that he'd seemed so out of place at the Grim. A quiet young man who sometimes stood in the same spot for hours, and who startled you with the harrowing seriousness of his conversation. Polak's only clear memory of him was that one time, while you could barely hear each other above the music and stoned women were tumbling all over you, Egon had told him why he'd decided to study geology. Something about a cave he'd visited as a boy, and that had made a big impression on him. You never saw him with a girl, and when Polak saw his name in the paper as a Dutch tourist who'd been murdered with a woman in a parking lot in Ratanak, his first thought had been: a woman in his life at last.

That boy's death had shocked Polak, and fascinated him, because he knew Egon had known Axel van de Graaf, yet the reports said nothing about drugs—and even more so when it turned out that Rosa Zinger was not the female victim's real name.

He had called Ratanak and started making inquiries around Amsterdam. Wagter had been a geography teacher, married but childless, and his wife had left him not long before. Polak dropped in on her at the offices of her hotel business: a surprisingly attractive woman, who had refused to talk to him, then talked to him anyway in the hall, begging him on the verge of tears not to make Egon a smuggler. She had no idea who the woman was he'd been killed with. The principal of Egon's school told Polak that Egon had needed money to go on a geological expedition. The apartment building where Egon had lived was close to the school. The nameplate in the entryway said: E. WAGTER, GEOLOGIST. Through the lace curtains, along the walkway on the fourth floor, Polak saw a tidy kitchen and a tidy little bedroom.

It made sense. Wife gone, financial problems, fourth-floor apartment in the suburbs—a perfect victim for the Doornenbosch route. Polak wrote a story about the murders in Ratanak, mentioning Doornenbosch, the Grim, and Axel van de Graaf.

When Polak answered his bell the next morning, Axel was standing on the stoop. Unshaven, in an old raincoat, alone. For the first time since the Grim, Polak saw Axel up close. He'd been writing about Axel all his life—it was as if his imagination turned real before his eyes.

"Polak," Axel said hoarsely. "Old gossipmonger."

"What are you doing here?"

"Scaring you."

"Oh. Then I guess you better come in."

Axel hobbled into Polak's living room and sat down at the big table.

There was no way Polak could act casual, not with this myth at his table. It was strange to sit across from someone who'd certainly thought about having you killed. You felt his power. If you threw a cup of coffee at him, you'd be shot dead on the street within a week.

But Axel was different from how Polak had ever seen him, or imagined him. He was slow, not so much the master of the situation, shaken.

"Off the record," he said.

"Fine," Polak said.

"What's this you're writing, Polak? Don't you ever learn? *In the old fraternity house on the Grimburgwal, Wagter met the future international drug dealer Axel van de Graaf.* Where do you come up with this stuff?"

"International, did I get that wrong?"

"Don't get funny. You say Wagter got to know me at the Grim."

"I write what I see."

"You write how you interpret what you see."

"He came there through you, he told me that himself. I remember that."

"So we already knew each other. Then you shouldn't write that we got to know each other there."

Polak was silent. This wasn't why Axel had come. This was the chitchat, the prologue to what he really wanted to say.

Axel pulled an envelope from his inside pocket and took a photo out of it. "This is where we met," he said.

He handed the picture to Polak. It was a little snapshot, in faded color, of a group of children at the ruins of a castle where a falcon hunt was going on. Polak recognized them both right away; their postures alone were enough. Axel was standing off to one side, his arms held out grotesquely to a girl who had a falcon on her arm and was looking a little frightened; Egon was watching, his arms folded, the way he'd always stood at the Grim.

So Axel had been a child, Polak thought. That was the most shocking thing about the picture. "Can I publish this?" he asked. "You'll get it back in one piece."

"Egon was my oldest friend," Axel said. "I didn't see him very often, but I loved him. He didn't love me, but you can't have everything. I knew him from when I was fourteen. From a vacation in Belgium, with Davy Youth Travels. Vacations like that create bonds for a lifetime. I'm completely devastated. You're the only one who knew him who I still see."

"We don't see each other."

"Oh no? These murders you blame on me, don't you call that seeing each other?"

"Do you know who that woman is?" Polak asked. He saw Axel's irritation immediately, right through the sorrow. He understood; Axel wanted to be seen as someone with feelings, and his question had reduced him to what he was: a drug baron, someone who knew criminal secrets, a supplier of sensational headlines. But Polak also saw that his question, the most obvious he could have asked, had flustered Axel—he'd come without having an answer.

So he knew.

"What do you care?" he said.

"Her family cares."

"And what do you care about that?"

"Was Egon Wagter in Ratanak because of you?"

"Yes," Axel said. He shook his head. He picked up the picture and looked at it. "I think I'm getting out. I'll tell you something. I've had a couple of bullets in me. And I have two daughters. You know what that does to you? It makes you wise. But that's completely different from what I always thought. I thought it would be a kind of mellowing, a realization that nothing really matters. But that's not it. Wisdom, that's being able to tell the truth by accident. Like making a kid. How many millions of sperm cells are there? Ten? Twenty? Each one's different, and you don't get to decide which one it will be. But what happens: it turns out you've made exactly that one person you love as much as you can love anyone. You've told the truth without trying. I've played a lot of tricks in my life, but the tricks I'm playing now tell the truth. By accident. That's wisdom."

He refused to say what he meant by those tricks, didn't mention the woman again, and only wanted to go on reminiscing about the Grim and that camping holiday in the Ardennes. After an hour he thanked Polak for the coffee, and for not having mentioned him back then in his piece about the people smuggling. Labored and limping, he headed for the door. Polak's hope that he'd leave the picture on the table was in vain.

ON AN OLD RIVERBOAT PIER along the Tonlé Kong, under canopies, was a busy restaurant. The pier stuck out into the dark river so far that boats bobbed by and underneath it, making it seem like a throne.

It was a dinner for four: Ambassador Kees Schilp and his wife, Dorothee, Mijnsherenland, and Polak. At George's recommendation, they'd ordered fish pulp as an appetizer: "Really fresh, straight from between the toes at Russei Keo."

Polak was to call them Kees and Dorothee, which was hard, because Mijnsherenland didn't. George was being rather quiet. It had all been his doing; he was the only one who actually knew a bit about Ratanakiri, and he'd done his work impeccably, but others would reap the profits. Polak had a good story, and Schilp had a mouthpiece—to what end, Polak wasn't completely sure. But there was no doubt that Mijnsherenland had shown him nothing, told him nothing, without Schilp's approving it first.

He couldn't shake the feeling that there was someone else present at their table, someone who wasn't there right now but could be back any moment: Oum Phen. A human being, whose glands diligently produced healthy juices and sent them to the appropriate parts of his body. He still had a few hours to live. Maybe he was sleeping. Maybe he was having a dream about something after his death, something that would really happen.

The main dish came with a platter of little birds, deep-fried in their entirety. Dorothee held them by the head and bit off the rest, George and Schilp ate them whole, and after a brief hesitation Polak did too.

Kees Schilp was a short man with a full clump of white hair, one of those rare sixty-year-olds in whom you can still see the child's face. Ratanak was his final post, and if there was one reason he and his wife longed for his retirement it was to be back in Holland for a winter cold enough for skating; as it turned out, they'd skated a lot of the same town-to-town tours Polak had.

Schilp felt Polak should go to the execution. The Ratanakirian flotilla wouldn't sail for Holland if he didn't—if only because not a single ship would make it past their own twelve-mile zone—but still it would be a bit unsporting. He'd made use of the whole circus that had been set in motion, even Sophal had cracked the whip for him, and it would be something of a letdown if he didn't show up for the Grand Finale. Besides, this was the crème de la crème: the execution of an innocent man.

"I have moral objections," Polak said.

"You have what?" Schilp said. "I asked you to call me Kees, not to use dirty language. You're a journalist, aren't you? A journalist gets in everywhere for free, especially into the cloakroom, so he can check his moral objections. You can have moral objection in your free time. That boy is being killed for *your* entertainment. You represent the Netherlands. Just like I do. Isn't that great? No dirty hands! When other people go to something revolting, they have no excuse, but you go to report how revolting it is. A journalist has to be able to stand a little stench and there's not much else he has to be capable of. An ambassador doesn't either, of course, all he has to know is how to dance the Viennese waltz. Can you do that?"

The Doornenbosch affair had happened during his ambassadorship. "An idiot, but brave. He didn't ask for a pardon, so he wouldn't have to hope anymore. That way he could take stock of what he was. Draw up the final balance. George paid him a few visits. The last one was two days before the end."

"Yes, he was brave," George said. "It was the dot that mattered, he said. He meant they'd given him power, that now he could decide what his life had been. He could put a dot at the end of it. Tie it up with a string."

"You're making that up about the string," Schilp said.

"No, he really said that."

"Nice," Polak said.

"Sartre, I believe," Dorothee said.

"That doesn't mean Doornenbosch couldn't have thought of it himself," Schilp said. "If something's of real value, a numbskull can come up with it, too."

He'd met Sophal a few times and found him fascinating. "Ruling is an art," he said. "Of all the things people are able to do, it's the most baffling to people who can't do it. When you see someone juggling Indian clubs, you can imagine that with a little aptitude and endless patience, you could do that, too. Build a cabinet. Skate around the country. Write a poem. Any of us can do that."

"Watch an execution," Polak said.

"Watch an execution while juggling Indian clubs," George said.

"But not ruling," Schilp said. "To kill, I can imagine that. But the contempt you'd need to *have* killed, not that."

"He's written poetry, did you know that?" Dorothee Schilp said.

"Yes, Dot, tell us about your letter," Schilp said.

In Paris, Sophal had published poems in a student magazine, in French. After he seized power they had been published in chapbook form, as a curio. Copies circulated in diplomatic circles in Ratanak, and Dorothee had one. Knowing that Sophal didn't renounce them, she'd talked to him about his poetry at a reception once, and his response had been friendly. That's how she'd found the courage to write him a letter about one of his poems, asking whether a pagoda in it was a certain pagoda in Ratanak. Sophal had sent her a handwritten reply, a piece of stationery written front and back, with *Tournez s.v.p.* at the bottom of the first page. He confirmed that he'd been thinking of that very pagoda and pointed out references to other specific buildings and spots in Ratanak, as well as a spelling mistake in her letter.

"Then my Dot felt the angel of death pass near." Schilp laughed.

"But he spared me," she said.

"Even though your crime was far worse than that of the poor devil who'll be losing his head tomorrow morning," Schilp said. "He was simply the wrong man in the wrong place, with the wrong twenty-dollar bill in his pocket. Oh, these terrible drugs. They cost Wagter his life, make no mistake about that. And that woman. And that beggar. And those two hoodlums. And Doornenbosch. And not one of them from the stuff itself. Why drugs have to be illegal, God knows. They create criminal employment, that's what they do. Prohibition was nothing by comparison. Come, don't let me forget to pour you another one."

After he had filled their glasses and ordered a new bottle, he asked: "Listen, you know this Van de Graaf, don't you? What's he really like?"

"I don't know him," Polak said. "I write about him."

Schilp smiled, and nodded. "Do you remember General Westmoreland?" he asked. "The American commander in Vietnam?"

Polak remembered him—and suddenly he also remembered, for the first time since, that he'd talked about him once with Egon Wagter, at the Grim.

"Do you remember what he said," Schilp said, "in the middle of that war? That people in these parts don't value human life like we do. The whole world was all over him. It was the most scandalous thing anyone had ever said about Southeast Asia. If you could point to three things that turned public opinion and finally made America lose that war, that was one of them. The naked napalm girl, the street execution, and Westmoreland."

"And that monk setting himself on fire," Dorothee said.

"All right, four. Have your monk, love. Of course, it was a blunder on Westmoreland's part. You can't say something like that when you're the one rubbing them out. But when you've been here for a while, Michiel . . . When you look around. Whap, a boy just gets the axe, to placate us. It's as easy for them as knocking back these birds is for you. And what do we do? We help them. I realize it's not the spirit of the times, but maybe we should take a good look at the quality of the life General Sophal is asking us to spend our millions on."

GEORGE DROPPED HIM off at the Holiday Inn at twelve and wished him luck. In his room, Polak poured himself a whisky and looked out over the dark river. This was precisely the view Wagter had had, although not as precisely as Polak would have liked: despite all efforts, including those of Mijnsherenland, he hadn't been able to get Wagter's room: he had the room next to it. In his story, he would have Wagter's room anyway.

He still didn't know what he was going to do. Maybe he still wouldn't know when they came to get him. He was afraid he'd throw up if he saw Oum Phen killed—that he'd always regret it if he didn't go.

It was impossible to stay in his room; he had to move. He went out again, left the hotel, crossed the plain to the city, stopped a scooter-taxi and said he wanted to go to the airport.

At the rotunda he climbed off and began walking back. Here and there people were still sitting around little fires. Now and then a scooter or a minibus came by. Lights were shining at the airport. He had to be careful where he walked; there were deep holes. He was being stared at. When he nodded, people nodded back. He felt safe, but he realized there was no reason why there couldn't be cutthroats around like the ones who'd butchered

Wagter and the woman. This was where they'd hung out, seen the two cars going to the parking lot, forged their plan.

Getting murdered too, that would add a nice touch to his article.

He saw the dark building and turned down the narrow road that led to it.

The lot was deserted. There were no cars. He heard the humming of a machine at the airport, a car, faint voices far away. He looked out across the field with the crooked palm. That was where the murderers had crept.

He went and stood on the spot where Wagter and the woman had lain. The bloodstains couldn't be seen now. It had happened such a short time ago—it was almost as if they should still be here—as if he, if he did his best, should be able to catch a final glimpse of what had happened.

The black void above the parking lot was like a high dark ceiling—like he was standing in an enormous cathedral. He felt how Egon Wagter and the woman had felt overwhelmed by that. They had come here as drug smugglers, but this place had made them belong together.

Compared to that, how petty and silly their prattling and laughter on that pier had been! The preciousness of Mijnsherenland's swimming pizza boys, his "General Suffering," of Dorothee's spelling mistake; that second-rate ambassador at his final post, wanting to vent his disgust at the two-bit country that had been palmed off on him—and who wanted to use *him* to tell its dictator: don't think you'll get off the hook so easily with your human sacrifice, old boy. If you kill them so readily, they're not worth our money! That crap about Westmoreland—the thought had occurred to him earlier in the day, too, but coming from Schilp it was the same as it had been with Egon Wagter, long ago at the Grim: despicable.

Egon Wagter, that had been something pure. That woman too. He'd seen it in the pictures: in those dead faces there was something regal that none of them could even come close to.

That's what his story had to be about.

His decision had been made, he noticed. He wasn't going to the execution. Those two were what mattered.

Oum Phen was an intruder.

# 4. Marcie's Gems

His parents had gotten married when they were twenty. "We were twenty"—how many times had he heard them say that? When he was little, as something funny, a naughty trick they'd played together, later more and more as: "We must have been out of our minds."

They had what few parents had: a picture of the moment they met. For as long as Arthur could remember, a framed enlargement of it had hung on the wall, the last few years in the hallway. You saw a big, crowded party, with people dancing and sitting at tables, a long buffet with food and beverages, a platform where a band was playing. At the edge of the platform, in the lower right-hand corner, a few boys and girls were sitting, David and Marcie side by side. Leaning over in front of David was a boy who seemed to be saying something; Marcie was staring quietly into the room, her face half-turned to a girl sitting on the other side of her. The next moment, according to the family legend that David always laughingly denied, he'd asked Marcie to move over a little—the other boy wanted to sit down too.

So it wasn't actually a picture of how they met, but of the last moment before they knew each other. Arthur had looked at it endlessly, at the faces of that boy and that girl, as if all the lives they could have led, and of which a moment later only one would be left, were still in them.

The next picture in which they were together was their wedding portrait.

They'd done it on purpose. Not the getting married itself—Jason, his older brother, was already on the way—but getting married while they were both twenty. David was six days shy of a year older than Marcie, and they'd picked one of the days between their birthdays. She was just past being nineteen; he was almost twenty-one. When it came time to say "I do," she'd fainted. But she came to quickly, and the whole thing went ahead. In the wedding picture, they looked like they'd won a trip to the moon.

Six months later Jason came; eighteen months after that Arthur arrived. By the time she was twenty-one, the same age he was when she disappeared, Marcie was a mother of two.

HE SAW HER for the last time in Osprey. He was majoring in journalism and English there; a little college town in western Massachusetts, an hour from Waterhead, the place where he'd grown up and where his parents still lived. It was on a Sunday at the start of the new school year, and the campus and town were full of the station wagons and pickups in which the freshmen hauled their things, and the music and the hammering from their open windows.

Marcie had suddenly called that morning to say she wanted to come by. He was almost out the door, on his way to go rafting with a few friends, and now he had to make sure he was back in time. She had clean laundry with her, and the old pair of binoculars that had belonged to her father and always stood on her desk. They'd been there long enough, she figured, he'd get them later anyway, so why not now? He made tea for them, and when he said he wanted to start doing a little more cooking, she sat down at his computer and typed in a recipe for herring-and-beet salad. They took a walk; he pointed out the offices of the *Osprey Sentinel*, where he'd be doing his internship, and on campus they sat for a while on one of the stone benches beside the fountain, looking at the little rainbows in the misty spray. She talked about a party she'd gone to as a young girl where some jerk had kept turning off the lights, and then suddenly she exclaimed that she had no idea why she was telling him that.

They ate at a restaurant in the old center of Osprey. He hated the question: "Is something bothering you?" but later he cursed himself for not having asked it that day. Something *was* bothering her. She was distracted. She talked about things that had nothing to do with the conversation, and she asked questions she had already asked. She hardly touched her food, and her laugh was put-on. She drank more wine than usual and told a breathless and confused story about Tucson, where she'd be going in a few days for the mineral show. She'd gone there often before, first to trade and buy stones, then in recent years to do business for Marcie's Gems, her rock shop in Waterhead. But now it was as if she were going for the first time and was a little worried about what was waiting for her there.

Sometimes, when she stopped talking, her face sank into the lost look he knew so well, but which lately contained a bitterness that made her older. And then the life would pop back into it, and she'd bring up old memories—about when they had no money, about the time he and Jason were messing with paint and a lady, Merle Ingraham of all people, the judge's wife, came by to pick up some cufflinks she'd ordered. "Dark red jasper from China. Oh, I was so angry that those stones weren't mine. You shook her hand. Her whole hand was covered with paint! And then you said: 'That lady's hand is all dirty!' "

For the thousandth time she pulled the face Merle Ingraham had pulled, and they laughed about it together. It was incredible how, from being so pensive and faraway, her face could light up just like that, the very same face suddenly becoming sweet and attractive. She had a special voice, young, fragile as a strand of copper, and, if you knew, still bearing the slightest trace of an accent. A voice made to cry: "Oh, how lovely!" Maybe not to drive a hard bargain in Tucson, Arizona.

As so often, it had occurred to him to say something about the day at Lake Munchie. He never had, for fear that doing so would make it something she might blame him for, something he should be ashamed of. Later it seemed he had been on the point of talking about it anyway, at the very moment she told him a secret.

"Shall I tell you something you don't know?" she said. "Jason was made the night David and I met. The night of the picture. Does that shock you?"

In a flash, before he could make sure he didn't think it, he thought: you're forcing yourself on me. We don't have that kind of closeness.

"Pretty much," he said. He didn't want to know: it was like being forced to watch as two strangers, the boy and the girl in that picture, went to bed together. It was more than he could imagine: his father as someone who'd gotten a girl into bed on the first night, his mother as a girl who'd let that happen. He'd always thought it had happened a few weeks later, and that Jason had been born prematurely—he was so naïve.

"Were you still a virgin?" he asked, irritated that she'd led him into such an unheard-of question.

"Yes."

"Doesn't seem like you."

"No, I'm a frump, aren't I?"

"Just because you don't lose your virginity on the first date doesn't mean you're a frump."

"But I am, a bit. I was then for sure. The kind of girl who never does anything that's dangerous or not allowed. A good girl. You make the grown-ups happy, you're an example, but sometimes it makes you angry because you know you're being a coward too. Everywhere you see children who aren't good, who do things they're not supposed to, and who are having more fun than you. Then you want that sometimes, too, to do something crazy and maybe dangerous, something that can change everything. You know you shouldn't, you're scared of it, but suddenly it's also the greatest thing you can imagine. And then you do it." She spoke forcefully, with almost the same anger she was describing, but when Arthur asked if she'd gotten pregnant on purpose that night, it seemed for a moment that she didn't know what he was talking about. She shot up out of what she was saying, and laughed her own laugh again. "*Jason* wanted me to be pregnant. Don't do that, Artie, have kids that young. We had to give up everything. Never only each other to think about. Never any time for silliness. Hey! I'm scaring you, aren't I? I've always been happy with the two of you, you know that! You promise me you'll always know that?"

On the walk back she put her arm through his, and at her car she pressed him against her. He smelled her, and felt her, and thought: my mother. Back in his room he looked at her lipstick on his cheek, and the crazy thought arose of taking a picture of it.

WHEN HE WAS fourteen and came home with a bad report card, David had demanded that he use the spring vacation to catch up on all the subjects in which he'd received less than a B. At the end of the vacation David would test him himself. Arthur had to cancel all his plans with his friends, put his books on the dining-room table, and spend his time studying there every day, from ten to four.

After he'd done that for a couple of days, sick from the sight of blue sky out the window, the voices of Jason and his friends going out in the morning, and furious with his ridiculously strict father, Marcie said at breakfast that it was a beautiful day, that he'd worked hard the last few days, and that now they were going to do something fun together, too.

"Arthur is going to study today," David said.

"Then the votes are tied," Marcie said. "Arthur has to cast the deciding vote."

"There is no vote; there is a decision," David said. But once he was out the door, Marcie told Arthur to close his books; they were going out, too. He didn't want to at first, afraid of the lying it would take, and of what David would do when he found out, but Marcie looked so disappointed that he went with her anyway. And with the top down they'd driven past David's office on the way out of Waterhead, into the radiant day, through woods, over hills, through towns they'd never been to before, and finally had never even heard of.

They stopped at a place called Lake Munchie, where in clear light the first sailboats of the year were shooting across the water. At a yacht harbor they rented a little fishing boat and took it out, put-putting and bobbing across the lake, getting in the way of the sailboats, inhaling the exhaust of speedboats and the other fishing boats, their hands dangling in the cold water. They went ashore on a deserted island in the middle of the lake, with a little beach covered with flat pebbles that were perfect for skipping. He wanted to teach her how, but she already knew. They threw, counted the skips, and it was as though their laughter and shouts skipped along behind. And suddenly, for the first time, he saw his mother as something separate, as a person, a woman in white jeans and a blue shirt crawling across the beach in search of good pebbles—someone who hadn't always been his mother, about whom you could wonder what she actually thought of it, of being Marcie Nussbaum, wife of David Nussbaum, real estate agent and contractor in Waterhead, Massachusetts, the mother of two boys.

In those days he'd had a crush on Charlotte Rohr, a girl from school, although later he wondered whether the crush hadn't consisted mostly of his memories of the talk he'd had about her that day with Marcie. She asked if he knew what he needed to about sex, and he'd laughed at her—David had told him a long time ago, when he was eleven.

"Good, then you're old enough to know the real secret," she said. "Sex isn't important. It's not something separate; it comes along with love, if it's there. A day like this is something you'll remember. Okay, not if it's with your mother. But you will if it's with your girl. That beats sex. There aren't many fourteen-year-old boys who know that. And be honest with Charlotte. If you have a crush on her, let her know. And if you think she's in love with you, too, grab your chance. Don't wait until it's too late.

Here's what you're going to do for the rest of the vacation. Every day, from ten to four, you're going to practice having a crush. And at the end of the week, I'm going to have Charlotte Rohr over to test you."

They took the boat back, got something to eat, and looked around in the village, and in a sporting goods store Marcie bought a new sort of throwing ring, a flat, open Frisbee. They went to the lake and threw it back and forth on a lawn along the shore. The thing sailed fantastic distances, pushed up or down suddenly by the slightest gust of wind; it hovered, flew back to the person who'd thrown it. They threw, caught, ran, and laughed, and later, when Arthur thought back on that afternoon, he was surprised they weren't throwing it still.

After one of his throws, the ring hovered for a moment above Marcie's head, dipped to one side, and dove into the water at an angle. It sank right away, so far from shore that they knew they'd lost it. They stared at the spot where it had disappeared, Marcie with an arm around his shoulders. "The evidence has been destroyed," she said.

They drove back to Waterhead, talking and singing at first, relieved that their cheerfulness could take the loss of the ring, but later, back in the world they knew, quiet—David was already in their thoughts.

When they got home, he was there. "Where have you been?" he asked.

And before Marcie could say anything, Arthur said: "I didn't want to. *She* wanted to go."

NOT A DAY went by but a candy wrapper, an autumn leaf, a spot of rust took him back to when he was little, because he'd seen their colors before the colors had names, in his mother's rock collection. It was a hobby she'd started as a child, and later pursued so stubbornly that it might have been her former life itself. She'd furnished part of the attic in their house as her rock room. There she had her books, her microscope, and her glass cabinets with the broad, flat drawers in which she kept her stones, in open boxes she made herself from big sheets of pink and pale yellow construction paper, cutting them to size for each separate stone, then folding and pasting them together.

Her table usually held her newest acquisitions, and always her first stone, the one she'd begun her collection with—a rough black chunk with a sort of green, luminous sugar cube in it: olivine basalt.

She had stones from all over the world and from every era; some of them were billions of years old. She'd once had him hold two stones in the same hand, and asked him what he felt. He hadn't felt anything special, but he remembered her excitement about those stones, three billion years apart, almost the full age of the earth. "Like having eternity in your hand! In one hand! Don't you feel that? Try it again!"

He and Jason had occasionally helped her cut and paste those boxes, and a few times they'd gone along to the abandoned quarries and cliffs where she looked for stones, but it didn't really interest them, and Sunday had gradually become a day when you said goodbye to Marcie in the morning, went fishing or sailing or swimming, and saw her again that evening, muddy and tired but with a rucksack full of stones, wanting nothing more than to disappear with them to her attic as soon as possible.

She bought and traded stones at fairs and through the mail, but she preferred hunting for them herself, sometimes on her own, sometimes with a mineralogy club from Osprey. Later, when Arthur went to high school and there was more time and money, those outings became expeditions; she went along on trips to Wyoming and Arizona, and a few times to South America, to Colombia and Brazil. From the garage usually came the growling and droning of what she called her time machine—the tumbler into which she tossed coarse stones, and which did in a few weeks what it took a river a million years to do; they came out smooth and neat as gems.

When Marcie worked on her stones, she forgot about time, and with a glance at the attic stairs David would say: "You need to be a goddamn fossil to get your mother's attention." Or he would hum "Heart of Stone" by the Rolling Stones, or ask her if there were stones that could cure you of rock fever. "I'm still looking for those," she'd say, "but all I find are stones that do the opposite." She had no use for any supernatural power of gemstones. Or for the word *hobby*. "There's only one hobby, and that's stamp-collecting. And I don't do that."

Dismissive as David was, Marcie had always clung calmly to her dream: having a rock shop of her own. You couldn't do that kind of thing in Waterhead, David had said. The only one who would buy anything there would be her, but in the course of the years his argument had shrunk to: "When the boys leave home." So when Arthur went to college and Marcie's parents died within months of each other, she used her inheritance to open her own shop at the nicest spot on Bertrand Street: Marcie's Gems.

At the opening, Marcie's Gems was a sea of flowers, with speeches and telegrams, and David had stood there laughing proudly, but Arthur had sensed what that laugh meant: anyone of any standing in Waterhead had a wife who studied or did something artistic, but his wife's hobby was worth a shop.

As they'd all predicted, or feared, or hoped, it didn't catch on. After only a few weeks, Arthur hardly dared to walk down Bertrand Street when he was in Waterhead, afraid the shop would be empty. And when there were people there, they were always the same ones—other rock hounds, like old Mr. Hammermacher, retired men who came to talk about their hobby and for whom Marcie made coffee and the occasional sandwich. They never bought a thing. The only paying customers were almost all children, who spent whole afternoons rummaging through her boxes of polished stones until they had a little sack full, for which Marcie charged them fifty cents. If they wanted, she even glued mountings on the stones for free, so they could make pendants. The big chunks of rock-crystal, the prehistoric fossils she had paid thousands of dollars for, remained on the shelf.

Arthur knew that Marcie's Gems wasn't meant to be just a store; it was also a studio for the jewelry she made, a mail-order house, and a meeting place for rock enthusiasts and mineralogists from all over—but there could at least have been a real customer now and then.

One time, when he was there and they heard the door swing open, Marcie had been unable to hide her joy, or her disappointment when it turned out to be Jason—a disappointment, he realized, she felt when *he* came too.

David said he'd been in a mineral shop in New York where they also sold animal skeletons and giant seashells, gemstones to help against rheumatism and headaches, zodiac stones, stones you could use to make someone fall in love with you. In the few minutes he'd been there he had seen four or five customers, and thirty or forty dollars worth of merchandise had crossed the counter. The time was right for it; people wanted that kind of thing. Why didn't *she* try to get customers by selling healing stones?

"If I came across a stone in my shop that cured AIDS and cancer at the same time, I'd throw it in the lake," Marcie said.

Arthur figured she must know what she was doing, because Marcie's Gems survived its first year, and its second. Maybe she'd inherited more than he knew, or maybe she was selling a lot by mail order. He didn't ask. Then, during a dinner at home with the four of them, an argument flared up between David and Marcie, one they'd obviously had before and that made it clear things were far worse than Arthur had suspected. Her inheritance had already gone into the renovation and the inventory; the annual revenues from Marcie's Gems weren't enough to pay one month's rent. David had done that for the first two years: two thousand dollars a month. Twenty-four thousand a year. Forty-eight thousand dollars in total. Arthur was shocked. And now one of David's business acquaintances who owned a chain of travel agencies across Massachusetts, but nothing in Waterhead, had his eye on the space on Bertrand Street and had offered to take it over from Marcie. David thought it was a good offer; Jason did too, and Arthur also realized it was the only sensible thing for her to do.

He'd never seen his mother so determined, so far removed from humor. The stones were a part of her, a passion. It had started when she was a young girl, and Marcie's Gems was the beacon she used to show it. The address was in magazines all over the world. Little magazines, but anyway, someone from Australia had come by once, someone from Poland too. They hadn't bought anything, but that was beside the point. Anyone who thought of Marcie's Gems in terms of money didn't understand a thing. And if they thought she was nuts, then they should think of the money that went into it as the bill from the nuthouse. They could afford it; their comfort wasn't at stake.

"Waterhead is a place for dumb materialists like me, not for sensitive souls like you," David said. "What matters is tomorrow, not a billion years ago. Stones are for building houses with. The time is coming when I'm going to cut the subsidy."

"Then I'll get it somewhere else," Marcie said.

SHE DISAPPEARED TWO days after the dinner in Osprey, on a Tuesday, at a little past three-thirty in the afternoon, from Platform 7 of South Station in Boston, where she'd arrived by train from Waterhead. The person who saw her there, Michael DaLiastro, a math teacher from Greenfield, had already seen her in Waterhead when she came into his compartment. She was carrying a brown suitcase that looked pretty heavy, and he'd helped her lift it to the rack. She looked familiar, but because he couldn't place her right away, he'd looked for a label with her name, but hadn't seen one.

They'd exchanged a few meaningless words and were silent for the rest of the ninety-minute trip, except when DaLiastro suddenly remembered where he knew her from.

He'd said something like: "Excuse me, but are you from Waterhead? Aren't you the lady from Marcie's Gems, on Bertrand Street?"

Marcie had said yes, and DaLiastro told her he had family in Waterhead, and that he'd been in her shop once.

"Did you buy anything?" she asked.

She didn't encourage any further conversation, and the rest of the trip she had sat reading *The Boston Globe* and her copy of

*Newsweek*, but mostly she'd stared out the window with what DaLiastro had termed "the look of someone thinking hard about something specific."

When the train pulled into Boston, Marcie took her suitcase down from the rack and said goodbye to DaLiastro. A few moments later he saw her out on the platform. She had put her suitcase on the ground, and he offered to help her. He had no luggage himself.

"Thank you, I'll call a porter," Marcie had said.

DaLiastro had said goodbye to her once more and walked on.

And there Marcie stood on Platform 7, her suitcase beside her, amid echoing boarding calls, the smells of coffee and rust, travelers bumping up against her, the rattle of trolleys pulling ribbons of little carts—but that was Arthur's Platform 7, months later, when he'd traveled in her footsteps and stood where she had vanished.

"That was where she was last seen," as the phrase went. But she had stood there a little longer, had hailed a porter, or had walked on once DaLiastro was out of sight. Hundreds, thousands of people had seen that, a whole station full of them, but there was no one who could tell Arthur, no one who had seen that she was standing on a launching pad from which she would be shot into a reality that was simply his, but which he couldn't know, no matter how desperate or angry he was.

WHEN HIS FATHER called to say that Marcie should have returned from Tucson two days ago but hadn't gotten in touch, Arthur's first thought was: the simplest explanation for this is that she is dead. It was as if he was being pushed into a forbidden chamber. If she'd been delayed or had wanted to stay a little longer, she would have let them know. So she couldn't let them know. She couldn't do something she normally could do. What did that mean? That she couldn't do anything anymore?

His thoughts could go no further.

David asked him to come to Waterhead that evening. Jason would be there too.


SHE STILL HADN'T shown up. Her time machine was growling in the garage. On the rack in the hallway her red coat was hanging. When he tried to catch her eye in the photograph, fear lunged in his throat: she was no longer there. Beside David was a black spot. At the same moment, he saw it was an empty knob on the coatrack hiding her face; all he had to do was move his head to see her. But for a second that black emptiness had been all there was: his mother didn't meet his father anymore.

Jason was already there. They hugged, frightened and clumsy. For the first time he felt the rasping of Jason's cheek against his. The house was filled with Marcie's absence: her plants standing there being green, her magazines on the table beside the couch, the spot where she'd tripped and spilled her coffee, the attic stairs. It was strange to see his father, a boy who had sat on a platform and was now standing here across from him and his brother, fumbling and unsure because the girl from the photograph was lost.

David had already gone to the police. It didn't look good. Or maybe it did. On the day Marcie left there had been a direct flight from Boston to Tucson, but she wasn't on the passenger list. Neither of the two travel agencies in Waterhead had booked her a trip to Tucson. Her trip was a fabrication, an excuse to do something they weren't supposed to know about. That made an accident less likely, but other bad things more likely.

Arthur could see her, at their dinner in Osprey. He had seen her know she wasn't going to Tucson, seen her think about what she really would do. Something dangerous and irresponsible, she'd said that herself. If he had asked: "Is something bothering you?" she would have told him.

Now that he had gone to the police, David said, there might be an investigation, so there was something he had to tell them, to be sure they wouldn't hear it any other way. He'd been having an affair. With Lilian Snead. For the last eight years.

Everything was different from what Arthur had thought— even though he knew right away that it was no different from what he should have suspected. Lilian Snead! It was unthinkable, and it made sense at the same time. Lilian Snead, of Harold and Lilian Snead, of Rudy and Ben, birthdays, school, hockey games in Boston, sailing.

"Does Marcie know?" Jason asked. *Does*, Arthur thought.

"Yes," David said.

"How does she feel about it?"

"She has her stones. She didn't care. I don't want to drag her through the mud. I don't want to drag myself through the mud. But we were twenty. We were too young. When you're twenty you should do silly things with your girlfriend, and when you break up, do them with your next girlfriend. Not go begging for a mortgage, building a crib. You have no time to work on each other. You can't help it, but at a certain point the falsehood enters your life."

"Don't let Lilian hear that," Arthur said.

"Not into my life," Jason said.

There was something else, David said. He'd paid the rent for Marcie's Gems for the first two years, but not after that. The third year Marcie had paid it herself. Twenty-four thousand dollars. He had no idea how she got the money. He'd asked her, but she had been vague. Something about stones. The police were going to look into it.

It's incredible, Arthur thought. We're sitting here, we're thinking things, and she's just dead. But what nonsense to think she's dead! Something simple is going on, but something equally simple keeps us from seeing what it is. The way you sometimes can't find what you're looking right at. Tomorrow everything will be back to normal. I call her, and she's there. And then I go to her right away.

But he couldn't think of a story she would tell him then.

Jason said that the evening before Marcie left for Tucson, she'd visited him and Janice. He'd found her nervous, and she'd given him a tie tack that had been her father's.

An icy fright filled Arthur's chest. She had said goodbye. First to her younger son, then to her eldest.


IT WAS as though a bucket of invisible paint had been thrown over Waterhead. Everything was "Marcie has disappeared": the patrol car of Officer Lace whose daughter had sometimes picked stones at Marcie's Gems, the Little Theater where the choir now practiced without her, the paper boy Tommy Serio who'd had newspapers in his hands that she'd had in her hands as well, the mailbox on the corner of the street where the Sneads lived, the one travel agency where she hadn't booked a trip to Tucson, the other travel agency where she hadn't booked a trip to Tucson, the trees along Petersham Road that she'd seen as her train left Waterhead.

A week went by, two weeks. It was absurd and incomprehensible. Your mother gone. Not there anymore. Like yesterday's clouds. The eyewitness reports followed one another quickly at first, like records being set in a new sport, but it ended with the math teacher. In an attic drawer, David found her passport. Jason had answered the phone one time at Marcie's Gems, and the other party had hung up right away. There was nothing they could do. They had to make a list of missing clothes. Using picture albums, they looked through Marcie's closets where pants and blouses lay being dead. They waited. Every year, fifty thousand people disappeared in America. Forty-nine thousand of them would return within a month. Of the other thousand, almost no one came back. That month still hadn't passed, but on which day did most of them come back? Had *that* day passed?

From long ago, something came up that it seemed he'd never thought of since. During a vacation, when he was nine or ten, the four of them had climbed a mountain. A long, hard hike along steep rocky paths that occasionally ran beside chasms, and David had forbidden Jason and him to leave the trail. They hadn't, but Marcie had, and at a certain point David had shouted: "Look out! You'll fall and kill yourself, and that would sort of spoil the vacation!"

No one had said anything; they'd just walked on, but for a moment Arthur had seen it all before him. They'd go on hiking, fishing, eating meals, and playing games, just the three of them, instead of the four of them, until they had to go back to school, but the vacation would be sort of spoiled.

Marcie wasn't there anymore—now what was he to make of that?

WATERHEAD DIDN'T BELIEVE Marcie had really disappeared. David offered ten thousand dollars for a tip that would solve the mystery, but the rumors went on. She had run away, to escape the demise of Marcie's Gems and leave her bad marriage behind.

Maybe she'd gone back to Holland, where her parents were from, and where she'd lived as a child.

Besides disbelief, Arthur also felt resentment, as if by suddenly not being there anymore Marcie was getting more attention than she deserved. She hadn't been the life of the party, hadn't won sailing races, hadn't flirted, hadn't waved banners when Jason competed in swimming meets. She had stayed home with her pebbles, preferring to talk about crystals with old men like Mr. Hammermacher—and now *she* was the one making the news as the biggest riddle in the history of Waterhead?

The big media weren't interested in her disappearance. "It's not exactly the Kennedy assassination," a television editor told Jason; America was full of bus stops, parks, department stores, discos where people had last been seen, people who, unlike Marcie, had no reason to disappear. She'd been up to something; all three of them remembered her saying that if she had to she'd get the money for Marcie's Gems somewhere else. And that's what she'd done, the police discovered; the rent for the third year had been paid in cash, right after an earlier trip to Tucson about which, like this last one when she'd disappeared, nothing could be found in her papers.

Where had that money come from? Had she borrowed it? It had to be black money, but black or no—why would anyone put any money at all into something like Marcie's Gems? Was it drug money? According to the police, drug dealers sometimes recruited helpers by lending them money and demanding repayment in the form of courier services. But how could someone like Marcie have contacts in that world? And if she'd borrowed money the first time she'd pretended to go to Tucson, what did this second trip mean? Had that been the smuggling? But then why hadn't she come back, or been arrested somewhere? Was she supposed to pay up, and had she tried to win time? Tried to borrow more? Had the lender demanded something in return and killed her when she refused? Sex? Marcie, at forty-three?

The investigation turned up nothing. The police couldn't rule out a disappearance, but that was all. They also thought Marcie had run away. Arthur wondered whether his telephone was being tapped, and David's and Jason's, too. Sometimes he was called down to the station to look at damaged suitcases, pictures of bodies, vacation snapshots. The three of them went to Boston together to look at clothing found in the storage room of a sex killer. The clothes were laid out on a long table, as at a flea market; undershirts, panties, bras, sometimes with the faint odor of perfume still in them, and during the drive home it occurred to him that those clothes had been lying there for years, and would continue to lie there for years, as a memorial to the Unknown Vanished Woman, to give everyone who was missing a woman the feeling that the case was being worked on.

Sometimes he thought it himself: Marcie had gone away. Maybe to a man, someone she'd met in her world of stones. Her marriage was hollow, her stone dream had fallen apart, he and Jason were grown. It had always seemed that she'd lost her way, being in Waterhead—that she had some other life, from which her life with them was only a temporary absence. David had played baseball and gone fishing with them, told them what time to be home, decided on their allowances and their punishments; *his* parents had been their grandparents.

Not being there went with Marcie.

But nothing that made her Marcie made it possible for her to have gone away without a word. He kept thinking about that moment on the platform, as if by thinking hard he could penetrate it and see where she went. Sometimes it was as though all he felt for her now was awe, because she'd been there at that magic moment. Sometimes he was angry at her. Always off with her stones, and now on his mind all day—who did she think she was? He was twenty-one, he had his studies, his internship, friends, hobbies, girlfriends; he had better things to do than be A Boy Whose Mother Had Disappeared. But whenever he saw someone running, he thought: she must have run one last time. When was that? Every phone call, every unexpected voice, every hand on his shoulder, for the rest of his life, would be Marcie.

She was dead or not dead, but he didn't know, so it seemed that this had yet to be decided—but how else could it be decided except by him knowing it? He hoped she would come back, with an unbeatable, disgusting hope he would have liked to tear out of him, the way Marcie had been torn away. Sometimes it seemed that his hope was the last bit of life left in her, and that he wanted to flog it out of her. Sometimes he thought he'd done that, that he'd actually stopped hoping, but when he asked himself what the difference was between this and her simply being dead, it was still that hope. She couldn't come back, but you could make up thousands of stories in which she *did* come back, stories that made sense. It was like the game she'd played with Jason and him when they were little. She would name two events, and they had to come up with a way for the second to result from the first. Because someone in Rio chokes on his pudding, someone in Paris buys a box of thumbtacks twenty years later. It was always possible; you could always come up with something that made sense. At the same time, you knew for certain that it hadn't happened and never would. A child on the beach takes a handful of sand and throws it. How much of a chance was there that those grains of sand would ever come together to form a handful again? None. But then how much of a chance had there been a thousand years ago? None either. Still, they'd come together. Something had happened that couldn't happen. That's how it was with everything. A step taken, a drop falling from a faucet, a bird sitting on a branch—never would it happen precisely that way again, never could it have happened. But if the world consisted of events that couldn't happen, then why shouldn't Marcie come back?

MARCIE'S GEMS ON Bertrand Street had stood there for a couple of weeks like a silent, somber culprit, the steel grating closed in front of the shop window with its stones, most of which had been there since the opening. After that a sign saying CLOSED FOR BUSINESS had appeared on the door, the shop window had been emptied, the sign had disappeared, and one day the homemade glitter letters MARCIE'S GEMS were gone from the storefront as well and in the window hung a poster saying: COMING SOON, A NEW ARCHIE'S TRAVEL PLANNER.

He lived, turned twenty-two, twenty-three, and maybe she lived, too—but she was dead. Sometimes he said that. The stones were sold, most of them to the wholesaler Marcie had bought them from, the choir sang, Mr. Hammermacher pulled a plastic bag over his head, Jason and Janice got married and went to live in Vermont, the Sneads moved to California, he had an article published in *The Boston Globe*, and David introduced him to Meg, a widow from Boston with two cute little boys; David wanted to move in with her there, and sell the house in Waterhead.

One evening, almost two years after Marcie had disappeared, Arthur went to Waterhead to talk about those plans. The picture was still hanging there, and now he found it fitting that his father and his mother, at the moment they'd made into the symbol of their marriage, had been strangers.

They ate at home; David cooked. They were cheerful and sentimental; it was probably the last time they would eat together in that house. David didn't try to hide how much he looked forward to his new life with Meg. They wanted to have children. He had his life ahead of him; he was only forty-six! Meg was peace and happiness, an oasis after the years with Lilian, the lying, the broken promises, their fights, the motel rooms whose pitifulness had seeped into their relationship.

*Lilian* was his disappointment in love, not Marcie.

"Have you ever wondered," David asked when it was already late, "how you came into the world? Or Jason, really, you weren't such a big deal anymore. Would you like to know the real story behind the picture?" The jovial and easy, the alcohol, had vanished from him, as if a plug had been pulled on all the rest and only this remained, the story of the moment that had decided their lives, and that had waited to be told one time—this time.

"She got pregnant that evening," Arthur said.

"You already know that."

"She told me in Osprey. That last time."

"Did she also tell you about the moving over?"

"No."

"I don't know what made her come up with that. Maybe to make the picture more telling than it was. It wasn't that way. We had already looked at each other."

It had never occurred to Arthur that the picture had a past, that the clothes the dancers were wearing had first been put on, that the man putting the cracker in his mouth had first picked it up—that David and Marcie, before they sat down on the edge of the stage, had walked over to it, had had lives.

"I saw her looking at me," David said. "I looked back. I thought she was nice. We had been standing close to each other, but I didn't dare talk to her. She did it. When I sat down on that stage I suddenly saw that she'd come to sit there, too."

The boy standing there was a friend, who hadn't asked if he could sit down, too, but who in fact had already been sitting there, and was excusing himself for a moment. When there was nothing in between them anymore, David and Marcie had looked at each other again, and laughed. She'd said to him: "Is your name David?" And he'd said: "Yeah, how did you know?" And she said: "I heard someone call you that." They had danced, stayed together for the rest of the party, and David had walked her home.

"It never occurred to me to get her into bed right away. I wasn't like that. And she didn't seem like that. We stood at her door, talking for a while. I said I'd like to see her again. I was almost going to shake her hand and walk away. Then she asked me to come up. The kind of father you probably think I am stops here. In her room I thought she was going to make tea, but she just said it: I want you to stay. This is where I stop."

"Why did she get pregnant?" He saw that his father was back at that evening, maybe for the first time in twenty years, and liked his mother, wanted to get to know her.

"We were green. Maybe because she wanted to belong some-where. With Jason and you, I was just part of the bargain. She hadn't been in America that long. At first I thought that evening meant I'd gotten her easily, but it meant I could never get her at all. By the time that sank in, we already had two children. It should never have happened, but that doesn't matter. You have to have a life. Whether you get it or choose it, you have to make the best of it. If you start off with love, it can go away. If you start without it, it can come. We started with children. I'm not angry at her. I like her. I love her enough to think it's too bad she never had a man she could love. I wish she'd come back, so we could split up in a decent way."

DAVID SOLD the house, and one day Jason and Arthur came to pick up and divide the last of Marcie's things. Arthur took the piece of olivine basalt she'd started her collection with; Jason chose the test tube in a little stand, with a moist, brown spot still in it—the pregnancy test that had proven his existence. Her papers, bills, letters, computer diskettes they put in boxes and folders, which they laid in a trunk David had bought specially for that purpose. No one had to say it aloud to know it was the funeral they needed. They brought up memories, laughed, drank, and looked at old pictures from before they'd known her, some of them from back in Holland. Marcie as a baby; proud in a classroom with a pretty dress; on a bicycle with a ribbon in her hair; with a falcon on her arm at a castle, a little afraid, with two boys, one of whom looked a lot like David; with her parents in front of their first house in Boston; on a bench in a park with the girl who'd been sitting beside her on the podium. It was crazy to see that girl anywhere but in that picture, as if a character in a movie suddenly stepped off the screen.

The picture itself they put in the trunk too. No one wanted it, and no one knew what else to do with it.

A little address book turned up as well, gilt-edged, colorful with curls and flower petals. Arthur recognized the young, neat handwriting, which could only be Marcie's, in which names and addresses had been written. Addresses in Holland, with the names of a few towns he knew: Amsterdam, Utrecht, Groningen, Haarlem, and also Hilversum, her birthplace. Inside the cover was a shiny sticker from the shop where she'd bought it, in La

Roche, in Belgium. These had to be the names and addresses of the children she'd been with in Belgium, on the vacation when, during a visit to a cave, her love of stones had begun. Wim Arkenbout, Frank Biemond, Steven Blaauw, Carla Blanken, Francien Calff, Axel van de Graaf, Menno Hoorntje, Petra Inkelaar, Kees de Jong, Yvonne Koster, Florrie Lanaker, Vera Lanaker, Sjoerd Mulder, Dorien Rademakers, Wim Setzekorn, Egon Wagter, Maria Welter, Dick Winnubst, Jan Zamel—strange and Dutch as those names were, it seemed after reading them once that he would never forget them.

David and Jason agreed that he should keep the booklet. It went well with the stone: they had probably been together in the bag she'd taken on that vacation to Belgium.

In the following days, whenever he looked at the booklet, and at the names and addresses in it, he was reminded of something Marcie had once told him about stones. They were almost all emptiness. There were only a few little dots of matter in them, like stars in the universe. She was that way too. What did he know about her? A few things. The nineteen children in that book, who must be in their forties now, knew completely different things about her. They must have been in that cave with her; they would be able to tell him what Marcie was like when she found something that would always hold her in its spell—and that had finally cost her her life. If he went to Holland, looked them up, talked to them, stars would be added; through her disappearance, Marcie would come into being as well.

But one day, without having known he would do it, yet as if carrying out a plan that had been there from the moment she disappeared, he got in his car and drove into the hills of western Massachusetts, until he found Lake Munchie. He was not going to Holland. Those children knew nothing about her. What Marcie had been, she'd been in Waterhead: his mother, who had thrown a ring with him.

He found the lake, the town, the lawn. He went down to the water and looked at the spot where the ring had sunk. It was probably still down there. He wouldn't try to get it out. It would only be thrown by her and by him. The ring would always be there. Until he was dead. A billion years.

He felt her close by—closer than she'd been since they'd been here together. He wasn't angry at her anymore. She could have her secret.

She had stopped being lost.

## 5. *The Cave*

THE BOY AND the girl discovered they were the only ones left. Between lunch and the visit to the cave, everyone was free: you could do whatever you liked. Some had gone for a short hike; others lay in the grass in front of their tents and read; on the long table in front of the main tent, a group was playing Monopoly.

But they, without noticing each other, had walked down to the river, where a narrow path was all that separated the campground from the water.

Suddenly they saw each other.

They were both a little startled and stood facing each other for a moment without saying a word. Some hikers were coming along, and they moved aside onto the stones at the water's edge. At this point the river was broad and shallow, the water flowed slowly. Rocks and small boulders stuck out above the surface, and little tufts of grass and weeds grew on a few dry gravel banks.

The sun was shining.

"Have you ever been in a cave before?" Marjoke asked.

"No, never," Egon said. "Have you?"

"No. But I think it will be nice."

"Me too," he said. "What do you think that Window is?"

"I wonder, too. Maybe something you can look through."

"It's a new cave, isn't it?"

"Yes, only three hundred and twenty-five million years old."

They laughed together at her joke; that's how old the lime-stone was in this part of the Ardennes. The caves at Hurennes where they would go that afternoon, twenty kilometers from La Roche, had been discovered two years earlier and only opened to the public that summer. They would be among the very first visitors.

They sat and looked out across the water. There were no swimmers in this part of the river; it wasn't deep enough. Farther along, a couple of fishermen were standing in the water, and two canoes came by; the people had to climb out and drag them over a shallow spot.

It was quiet on the water again. The fishermen made no sound; the canoes had disappeared from sight. On the other side was the hill where they would go blueberry picking that evening. People were walking way up there, but you couldn't tell if they were from Davy.

They threw pebbles in the water and looked at the rings which, as they spread, began moving along with the stream.

"You speak really good French, don't you?" Egon said.

"Aw . . . ," Marjoke said.

"No, really, I think you do."

"I've been on vacation to France with my parents a few times. I like it there. And we get it at school."

"What class are you in?"

"I'll be in the third."

"Me too. Gymnasium, right?"

"Yes, gymnasium," Marjoke said.

"Me too. Then we're probably the same age. I'm fourteen."

"Me too."

They laughed, as if all these things they had in common made it incredible that the two of them had never sat together beside the river like this.

But there were differences too. Her favorite subjects were French and drawing; his was physics. His father was an architect; hers a cyberneticist. He had never heard of that profession, and Marjoke didn't know much about it either, except that it was a branch of mathematics that had to do with giant computers. As they discovered these differences, they said "oh, right," in a forgiving tone—after all, they couldn't have *everything* in common.

She was from Hilversum, and that was sort of something they had in common, too, because that's where Axel, Egon's tent mate, was from. But that was no coincidence; Marjoke's father worked at the hospital where Axel's father was the director. Their parents had heard from each other about Davy Youth Travels.

"So you already knew Axel," Egon said.

"Ever since we were little."

"What was he like then?"

But from the face she made he could tell she didn't want to talk about Axel, that she didn't like him, but that she didn't want to come out and say so to him, Axel's friend for this vacation.

They told each other about their houses, their parents, the brothers and sisters neither of them had. America, Marjoke said, was the land of the future for cybernetics. Her father had made a computer language specially for the medical profession, and it was used in hospitals in America, too. He'd had a few offers to go and work there. Sometimes her parents talked about emigrating, but she hoped they wouldn't.

While they were sitting there talking, Egon had picked up some flat pebbles, and now he stood and skipped a few across the water. Some of them bounced seven or eight times. Marjoke tried it too, but she couldn't do it right away, not until Egon showed her how to hold the pebble between your thumb and your bent index finger, and then give it a spin right when you let go. "Yeah!" they shouted at the same time when her first stone skipped a few times, and together they imagined how a stone like that might skip the entire length of the Ourthe—but what did the Ourthe empty into again?

"Into the Meuse?" Marjoke said.

"The Rhine, isn't it?" said Egon.

"Naaw!" She laughed. "That's all the way over there!"

"But the Meuse empties into the Rhine, doesn't it?"

"Yes, with a couple of rivers in between. Not really."

"It's not very nice for a river if it never gets to the sea itself," Egon said. "If it only gets to go along with another river."

"You're right," Marjoke said. "Shall we help the Ourthe? We can build a dam, we'll just give it a detour."

"We'll make the Ourthe empty into the Rhine!" Egon said.

"Straight into the sea!" Marjoke said.

"Yeah! Then when we have a geography test, we can just fill that in. And if they count it wrong, then we bring the teacher here to see for himself. The Ourthe meets the sea at Noordwijk!"

"Amsterdam-on-the-Ourthe!" Marjoke said.

"*Hilversum*-on-the-Ourthe!" Egon said.

They doubled over with laughter at that, and when they were done laughing they took off their shoes and socks and waded into the water. One meter out, a big rock was sticking up above the surface, and they began tossing stones between it and the bank. Before long those new stones were sticking out of the water, but because they kept taking them from close to their dam, they undermined it while they were building it, and a few times it started to fall apart. Egon began bringing rocks from upstream, and Marjoke placed them carefully in the dam, which was becoming stronger now and actually holding back some water. Faster than the rest of the Ourthe, it flowed sideways along their dam, past the big rock, until it could flow along with the Ourthe the way it always had been. Right behind the dam was an eddy now, where strings of froth and little pieces of wood drifted around without going any farther.

They had already changed the Ourthe a little.

They continued their work on the river side of the big rock. Egon got the stones, Marjoke placed them in the new section of their dam. It was deeper there, and the stronger current they'd created made it harder to build. They came up with the idea of laying buttresses, little piles of stones right behind the dam, to support the ones in the dam itself. Marjoke gave orders to Egon to find the right stones; he gave her instructions for building. It was precision work; one wrong stone and Hilversum and Amsterdam would never lie on the Ourthe!

It went slower than it had along the bank, stones kept rolling back into the water, but there was no way they'd give up. The dam already stretched a good meter from the big rock toward the far side, and it was already strong enough to stand on carefully, when a call came from the shore.

It was Kees, the counselor. "Hey, where have you two been?" he shouted. "We're going to the cave. Or did you forget about that?"

Without noticing it, they'd spent more than two hours on their dam.

AN OLD STEAM TRAIN with wooden benches took them from La Roche to Hurennes, through tunnels and past fields, but mostly right along the Ourthe, running unawares in its old bed. Egon and Marjoke occasionally caught each other's eye, and when they did they nodded briefly at the river, guardians of a secret.

At Hurennes they had to hike from the station to the cave, straight up along a narrow path, dark under trees that overshadowed it completely. There was singing, and shouting that it was too far and too hard, until the trees opened up and they were standing at the edge of a pasture with haystacks and cows, as if here, at this elevation, the flatlands began again. At the edge of the pasture was a little brick building: there was the entrance. They had to wait for a group that was still in the cave and they looked around in the building where you could buy ice cream, cold drinks and postcards, beautifully colored minerals, fossils, and guidebooks and geological maps of the area, too.

But that would have to wait; the other group was coming back up. Their visit to the Caves of Hurennes was beginning.

Down a sort of cellar stairs the Davy group descended, until they came to a heavy door. When the guide opened it, a cold draft brushed their bare arms and legs. As far as you could see, in the weak light from bulbs strung at intervals along the stone ceiling, the stairs went down. The steps were wet and slippery, on some of them were puddles, as though it had been raining here. Occasionally you heard the plunk of a drop falling in one of those puddles.

At the bottom of the stairs the guide turned a switch, and a sigh of admiration, like at a fireworks display, ran through the group. They were standing in an immense vault, high as a cathedral. On the ceiling hung all kinds of stone growths—cones, veils, elephant ears, tatters like the wash in an Italian alleyway. There were pillars from the floor to the ceiling, and everywhere you saw the beginnings of new pillars, stalagmites on the floor, stalactites from the ceiling.

With a heavy French accent, at which there was some muffled laughter, the guide told them that the limestone of Hurennes had been formed three hundred and twenty-five million years ago, from the skeletons of plankton in seas that had once been here. Limestone dissolved in water; the caves were created by water forcing its way in, from rain, and from rivers. If they looked closely they would see that, from some of the cones, drips were hanging that had seeped through all that rock, and that in turn would add an infinitely small bit of limestone to it. When one of those drips fell, the same thing happened on the floor. They could imagine that a pillar like that didn't get there overnight; the stalactites and stalagmites took a couple of hundred years to grow one centimeter.

One centimeter! A little cone like that on the ceiling, a little baby pillar on the ground, was already centuries old. How many thousands, hundreds of thousands of years must it take for the two to come together and form one pillar?

Marjoke was close to Egon.

"Scary," she whispered. "All that time!"

They followed the guide farther into the darkness, which stopped being darkness every time he turned on the light in the next vault and switched off the previous one. Until only a light went out, and no new light came on. Suddenly they were standing in the dark. There was giggling and whispering, Axel laughed his high laugh, and someone shrieked; it sounded like Florrie. "Guys!" Kees said.

If they were quiet, the guide said, really quiet, they would hear something very special. They all held their breath; even Axel was silent. After a little while a rustling became audible, far away, like the sea in a shell.

"What you're hearing now," the guide said, "is an underground river. More than ninety-nine percent of all the earth's freshwater is under the ground. This is one of the invisible streams that give the Ourthe its water. That water will finally flow down the Meuse, the Waal, and the Rhine into the North Sea."

"So he thinks," Marjoke said.

The guide turned another switch, and now they saw that they were standing at the edge of a deep, green pool. It was as though it couldn't have a bottom, so transparent and luminous was the green.

But the best, the guide said, the most amazing thing, was yet to come: the Window of Hurennes. No other cave in the world had anything like it. He led the group into the next vault, but when he turned on the light there, it looked just like the one before.

"Here you can see time," the guide said. He pointed to a wall where the grayish white of the limestone shifted along a sharp line into dark black rock with glistening green spots in it: olivine basalt. This type of stone had been named Hurennite. Up at the shop they could buy a piece as a souvenir. It wasn't expensive.

The vault where they were standing now had been formed precisely along a fault plane between the limestone and a basalt layer, which was a hundred million years older. That older layer never came to the surface, but here they could see it anyway. This was called a Geological Window. It was a hole in time, a look at a past that was hidden everywhere but at this one little spot. All other known Windows were found on the surface; this was the only Window in a cave.

"In a museum of antiquities, you are not allowed to touch things," the guide said. "But here you may. Place your hand on the fracture, and you will be bridging a hundred million years." But even during the last part of his explanation there had been talking and laughter, and now children started walking away, some of them after hardly touching the line. "If that's a window, it could use some wiping," one of them said.

Egon went and stood at the wall. He placed his hand on the border between black and white. Marjoke stood next to him. She put her hand beside his. They looked at each other. They were incredibly close to each other.

HE WOULD GO up to her. Say he wanted to pick blueberries with her. But she had to help with the chores, so he went ahead to the crossing, where they would all go later to get to the blueberry hill. Balancing on the stepping stones, he walked to the other side. A little farther along, at the bend in the river, he saw their dam. He wanted to take a look there, too, but he must have been dreaming, because here came the others already, with baskets and sacks for the berries. Marjoke was walking alone, and he realized the blunder he'd made—while he was down here, some other boy could have asked her. Fortunately that hadn't happened—or if it had, maybe she had said she was already going with him.

He hurried back across the stones. Stupid of him to be so nervous about it. All they were going to do was pick berries. And everything made it seem that she liked him, too, that she was counting on going with him! She was already smiling at him, and he was going to put out his hand to her, but suddenly Axel was there, pushing Vera out in front.

"Hey, Egon," he shouted. "Listen."